**"Exactly how do I fit into this?"**

"It makes everything more complicated, because while I know you're here only for a job, I felt something," Ana said. "A spark. I had thought that you felt it, too, and perhaps that there would be... more."

"More?" Chance echoed, his voice low, and rougher in a way that rubbed over her skin.

She smiled a little. "I've had lovers. I have a career. I don't intend to get married or settle down, not anytime soon. But I'd hoped there could be more between us, at least while we were here in Mexico."

Chance seemed to consider what she'd told him, and then stepped even closer.

"Thank you, Ana, for the truth. Here's mine," he said softly, lowering his head and taking her mouth in an unexpected kiss that wiped everything else from her mind.

Chance's hands were at her waist, pressing her close as he walked her back against the broad trunk of a tree in the garden, trapping her against it as the kiss deepened. She wanted him, more than she had known.

And now she knew that he wanted her just as much....

Dear Reader,

We have exciting news! As I'm sure you've noticed, the Harlequin Blaze books you know and love have a brand-new look, starting this month. And it's *hot!* Don't you agree?

But don't worry—nothing else about the Blaze books has changed. You'll still find those unforgettable love stories with intrepid heroines, hot, hunky heroes and a double dose of sizzle!

Check out this month's red-hot reads....

I hope you're as pleased with our new look as we are. Drop by www.Harlequin.com or www.blazeauthors.com to let us know what you think.

Brenda Chin
Senior Editor
Harlequin Blaze

# His Kind of Trouble

## Samantha Hunter

HARLEQUIN®

entertain, enrich, inspire™

Recycling programs
for this product may
not exist in your area.

ISBN-13: 978-0-373-79735-6

HIS KIND OF TROUBLE

www.Harlequin.com

**Printed in U.S.A.**

## ABOUT THE AUTHOR

Samantha Hunter lives in Syracuse, New York, where she writes full-time for Harlequin Books. When she's not plotting her next story, Sam likes to work in her garden, quilt, cook, read and spend time with her husband and their dogs. Most days you can find Sam chatting on the Harlequin Blaze boards at Harlequin.com, or you can check out what's new, enter contests or drop her a note at her website, www.samanthahunter.com.

## Books by Samantha Hunter

### HARLEQUIN BLAZE

 *The HotWires
**American Heroes
 †The Berringers

To get the inside scoop on Harlequin Blaze and its talented writers, be sure to check out blazeauthors.com.

Other titles by this author available in ebook format.

To new friend and author Melissa Cutler, who inspired me with her travel stories to set this story in the Yucatan; it was fun, and now I want to visit.

To my editor, Kathryn Lye, for all of her hard work on my books, and to Blaze senior editor Brenda Chin, who came up with this great set of series titles. Thank you both!

As always, to Mike, with love. You make every day an adventure.

# *Prologue*

JONAS, GARRETT, AND ELY Berringer—along with their cousin and new member of the team, Luke—were stunned as they watched the plasma TV screen together. Ana Perez, the petite Mexican chef on the screen, ordered her kitchen staff around with the authority of a military general. Garrett felt his spine straighten as he listened to her.

The rant that ensued when a contestant on the show messed up was epic. The people in the kitchen—many of them large, serious-looking men—paled. Perez didn't bother cleaning up her language all that much—though a good deal of it was in Spanish—when someone's sauce was cloudy, or muddy, or their vegetables were limp.

"Man, I bet the asparagus isn't the only thing going limp in that kitchen," Luke offered, earning a chuckle.

*If You Can't Take the Heat...,* Ana's Mexican cooking show, was a hit, and her fiery, unforgiving disposition was one reason why. It was also the probable reason why someone had been harassing her—at least, that was the theory.

"Holy—" Garrett whispered, unable to take his eyes

from the screen. "I didn't think they would let you say that on TV."

"It's cable, but watching this, it's not hard to believe that someone wants to knock her off," Jonas added as he smothered a grin at his older brother's glare.

Shutting the television off and turning on the lights in their small conference room, Garrett, the oldest and the one who ran most of their business dealings, turned to the others.

"This is a big opportunity for us. Getting a foot in the door with celebrities is tough, and the studio is desperate after her current detail quit. We can make some good money if we pick it up now," he offered enticingly.

"So she didn't hire us?" Ely asked.

"No. She's not really thrilled about having a bodyguard. The production company is the boss. She's their investment, and they want her safe for the new season. Two weeks in Mexico. Not so bad."

"Right, that's why you're jumping on it for yourself," Ely said, leveling his brother a look. "I'm out. Lydia and I are heading back to Montana end of the week. I have a class starting in two weeks."

Ely and Lydia were moving to Montana, which had been a shock to everyone, but Garrett was happy for his brother. They all were. Ely would work special assignments when they really needed him, but otherwise, he was pursuing a new career as an architect, and Lydia was opening a new branch of her tattoo shop.

Jonas shook his head before Garrett could even speak the words. "Sorry. You've already got me booked, remember?"

Garrett had forgotten, and grimaced.

Everything was changing for the Berringer brothers, and for the better. Several successful cases had landed them more business than they could handle, and Garrett was starting to feel the pressure. He'd have to start interviewing some new bodyguards, and soon. All three brothers had met special women, and all three had walked down the aisle or were planning to; it made everything a lot more complicated.

"I like Mexico and pretty women," Luke volunteered, but all three brothers shook their heads. Their cousin Luke was the latest addition to the group, but he wasn't ready to take on anything this high-profile or this dangerous. His specialty was white-collar work, anyway. Garrett hadn't imagined him out on jobs so much as working from his computer.

Garrett blew out a breath and accepted his fate.

"Well, Tiffany is starting the FBI forensics course I gave her for Christmas tomorrow, so she won't be around much, anyway. Looks like I take the bullet on this one," Garrett said grimly, looking up at the TV. "Maybe that attitude of hers is all for the show," he added hopefully.

Before any more was said, the door opened, revealing a surprise for all of them as Chance walked in.

"Hey, what are you doing home, little brother?" Jonas asked.

"I thought you were off skiing until after the New Year," Garrett chimed in but was nonetheless glad to see his youngest brother and welcomed him with a handshake and shoulder-bump.

"Logan broke his leg and had to be airlifted off the mountain. It was a mess, multiple compound fractures. Was a tough time getting him off the mountain and through surgery. By the time he was out and set to go home, I decided to call it quits and come back here. So what's going on? What are you all watching?" Chance asked, glancing at the TV.

The three brothers all looked at each other, then at their youngest sibling with wide grins.

Chance stared back. "What?"

"You have great timing. We were just thinking about turning down a job because none of us are available," Garrett said, fingers crossed.

"No way. I'll do it. What's the job?"

It was just like Chance to say he'd do it before he even knew what it was. Just what Garrett had been counting on. Garrett took a photo of Ana out of a file and pushed it across the table, watching his youngest brother's jaw drop. "The show tapes in New York, and she's leaving for Mexico the day after tomorrow. If you can get there tonight, even better. Everything you need to know is in the file."

Garrett watched his brother's reaction and knew Chance was already hooked. Chance couldn't say no to a hot woman, and Ana might be crazy, but she *was* hot.

"Beautiful woman with a threat on her life. It's custom-made for you," Ely chimed in.

Chance whistled at the photo, picking it up for a closer look. "Who'd want to harm a hair on this gorgeous creature's head? I'm definitely your man," he said to the photo more than to his brothers.

Garrett's grin widened. "Couldn't have said it better myself."

# 1

IT WAS THE DAY AFTER Christmas, and Ana Perez had worked through the holiday. Something that had happened two years in a row since she'd started hosting her reality show, *If You Can't Take the Heat...*

She'd been taping for the next season every day, non-stop, and while the group of chef-wannabe contestants for this season were the best they'd ever had, that came with its own problems. Soon they would start their short midwinter hiatus before the taping of the finale. She was alone on the set, reviewing her notes concerning the contestants' progress so far.

Unlike the shows where players were voted off or eliminated by failing a task, on *If You Can't Take the Heat...* the decision about who won was always Ana's. That had been written into her contract; that had been a deal breaker. She wasn't about to have her name associated with any chef recommendation that wasn't from her directly, so winners could not be selected by chance or by personality wars. The tide was turning, however. The studio executives were being more intrusive in the show's format, and in her life. Sometimes the producers wanted her to do stupid things—like a staged food fight on one show. Ana won a lot of those battles, but not all of them. It seemed as if the more famous she became, the less control she had over her life.

Every meeting was deteriorating into a fight. Recently, they were debating taking control of the final decision away from her.

Luckily, Ana was a fighter. No way was she giving that up.

There was a lot of pressure on her, not just from the studio but from the audience and from the contestants. Not everyone agreed with her choices; some were almost pathological in letting her know what they thought, if her email or the show's blog were any evidence.

The recent harassment she had been experiencing was also the price of success. Ana didn't pull punches or take it easy on her contestants, though she was rarely genuinely angry with them. Her tough treatment of them was in part for ratings—viewers liked the conflict— and also because she was a perfectionist who demanded the best of them.

Ana couldn't be a best friend to the people she was judging—better that they were afraid of her or didn't like her than have them feel hurt or betrayed when she didn't choose them to win. She'd made that mistake the first season with someone who had mistaken their friendship for an automatic win. Ana took a deep breath, shaking the memory off. It was wearying, sometimes, to say the least.

If nothing else, every person on the show would benefit simply from the exposure of being here. Most got good job offers afterward, even when they didn't win. For the ones who showed real promise, she sometimes connected them with someone who might further their training, behind the scenes. For Ana, it meant a big pay-check to help people back home in Mexico, and security for her and her family.

That was important enough to put up with all the rest, she reminded herself.

Shifting her attention back to the files on her lap, she reached for the glass of wine she'd poured before sitting. It had been the pairing for the smoky *molé* she'd had contestants working on for the past two days. Viewers saw only the final taping of the show, but Ana worked with contestants in the kitchens every day, all week long, teaching. Preparing.

Making *molé* was an art in the small town on the Yucatán where she had lived until she turned twenty and came to the United States to attend cooking school, eight years before. The complex cooking project had allowed her to educate people about her home country and their traditions, as well.

Bailey Knowles was the front-runner in her mind so far, a young woman from the Bronx who had no formal training and an uncanny ability to match tastes, textures and combinations in extraordinary ways. But she also had no classical culinary background and no interest in accumulating one.

Still, Ana felt that training was an important companion to natural talent and couldn't help but hesitate at selecting Bailey as her winner for the season.

James Benois was next in line, an older contestant in his forties, making a comeback after being laid off from his corporate job two years before. He had a culinary education that he had let lapse in the eighteen years since he'd earned the degree, choosing to make a steady paycheck with a technology firm. Still, his story resonated with viewers and with Ana. He was good, solid and dependable, though not extremely creative. That could change as he loosened up a little. He was too anxious to please, perhaps too laid-back to run his own kitchen. Kitchens were busy, difficult, stressful places to work—a head chef had a lot of responsibility—and James had to be able to show he could stand up to the worst of it. Still, his easygoing manner was calming, and Ana found the contrast a positive one.

There were four more, all having their own pluses and minuses, some exceptional in a particular way but less so in others.

She stared down at Lionel Jenkins's photo. She didn't have many notes on Lionel. She knew his type and she didn't like him on principle. From a wealthy Philadelphia family, Lionel was an excellent chef with perfect references and education. He could handle himself in the kitchen—she'd give him that—and he was very handsome, which was a big score with female viewers.

Too bad he was also a total jerk. He cared about nothing but money and ambition, and while he could have walked into a lot of high-level chef positions, or probably have even started his own restaurant with his family's money, he'd pulled strings to end up on the show. He was using them for the free promotion, a stepping stone in his career. He'd as much as told her so, which was why he was resistant to her criticism.

Granted, that attitude would probably be a benefit when he ran his own kitchen—many chefs had egos bigger than their hats—but Ana wanted her winner to care about more than money. Ambition was important, but so was some demonstrable caring about food, community, the craft...all of it.

Rubbing her eyes, she took a breath and closed the files. At least they were done with the taping, and now she only had to review all of the shows, interview her contestants one more time and make her decision. But for right now, she was ready to go home.

Her heart swelled at the thought. She loved New York and the winter, which she had never known as a child in Mexico. But it wasn't home.

*Soon,* she reassured herself. Two weeks of heaven, where things were lovely, warm and welcoming. Where she could be herself among friends and family, with no stalkers or studio executives scrutinizing her every move.

She missed having her own small cooking show, where she had happily instructed others to make authentic Mexican dishes. When she had started doing it in college—*Ana's Kitchen*—they'd had one camcorder and had held the show in the dorm kitchen, uploading it to the internet.

It took off, becoming one of the most highly rated cooking shows online. She'd then been offered a real cable TV show for the Cuisine Channel and, ultimately, the reality TV gig, *If You Can't Stand the Heat...* And here she was. The show had been on for only two years, but it felt like ten.

With a tired sigh, she packed everything up to head back to her dressing room and call it a night. A glance at her watch told her that it was actually close to being the next day.

She hadn't realized it was so late. Ana had meetings in the morning—they were foisting some protective detail on her because of the harassment issue—and she was supposed to come in and meet whoever was assigned to protect her over the hiatus.

She had no intention of agreeing; she planned to leave all of this behind her. Whoever was bothering her would probably lose interest in her over the break. Things like this flared up from time to time; it was part of the business. She received all kinds of crazy letters; if she took all of it seriously, she'd have no time to cook.

Walking down the dimly lit hall of the soundstage, she dismissed the thought. She entered her dressing room and closed the door behind her. Turning, she found a man sitting on the sofa. Immediately, her fingers fumbled for the doorknob as she dropped her files, and panic rose tightly in her throat.

"Ana," he said, and she spun to face him.

Her stalker.

He wasn't what she expected, to be sure.

A tall, broad, *huge* man with dark blond hair—and incredibly clear green eyes—looked at her with curiosity more than anything else.

Her phone. She fell to her knees, looking for her phone among the papers, and gasped in relief when she had it, pounding out security's number, her eyes on the intruder.

He didn't seem concerned.

"This is Ana. I'm in my dressing room. There's a man here. He's broken in. Please come now," she said urgently, not taking her eyes off the guy, but then she realized she was talking to a recording.

Her stomach dropped. Where was the night guard?

The green-eyed hulk blinked at her, then smiled.

"You're Ana Perez," he said calmly, taking a seat in the chair across the room, crossing long legs as if he had nothing to worry about.

Her eyes searched desperately for something to defend herself with, landing on a little red box on the wall.

As she dived for it, he stood, putting his hand out.

"Ana, no," he said, but it was too late.

She pulled the fire alarm and let it ring.

"I am. And you're about to be arrested," she said. "No way am I letting you out of here, no matter what you do to hurt me."

He sighed and shook his head.

"Ana, I'm not going to hurt you. Quite the opposite. But security won't be here anytime soon. The fire department will, but not security."

"And why's that?" she asked, fearing he had done something horrible to Ben, their night guard. Ben had lost his wife the year before, was near retirement and was celebrating the arrival of his first grandchild. Ana chatted with him every night before she left. He was a sweet, good man.

"What did you do to Ben? If you hurt one hair on that man's head, I'll—" she threatened as she took a step forward, then stopped. She had no idea what she would do.

The man reached into his pocket, pulled out a small black phone. "Your security guy left his phone on the front desk when he went to the men's room," the man said laconically. "The studio definitely needs to beef up the night watch. It was easy as kittens to get in here. I could have been anyone. Someone who does want to hurt you."

She blinked. "What do you mean?"

He walked toward her and put out his hand, and she had another chance to appreciate the solid mass of muscle that allowed him to move with a dangerous kind of masculine grace. Cocky, self-assured, powerful and not at all worried about being caught. Certainly not afraid of her.

She was dismayed to hear a panicked squeak emit from between her lips.

As if he was dealing with a frightened animal, he bent down to her level.

"Ana, my name is Chance Berringer. I'm your bodyguard," he said, holding out his hand just as she heard the sound of heavy footsteps landing outside the door.

CHANCE STOOD AT THE END of the hall near Ana's dressing room, watching her sign autographs for some of the firemen who gathered around. The least she could do, she said, after dragging them out for a false emergency. One guy suggested filming their show at the firehouse one week, feeding all the guys, and Ana seemed to seriously consider it.

The men were rapt. Chance didn't blame them. She was even more striking than in her picture.

Petite—not more than five foot two, tops—Ana Perez packed every inch of her small frame with succulent curves and intriguing angles that he enjoyed studying as she worked the crowd.

*Too bad she's a client,* he thought with a sigh. Hands off. Chance liked women—lots of women, all women, in all shapes and sizes and colors—and he never experienced a shortage of female company. But clients were always off-limits when they were on a job.

Well, unless you counted how all of his brothers had met their wives and current significant others, he thought with a smirk. All of the women had been principals, or clients needing protection, when they'd met.

Not that Chance was looking for a wife. Women were wonderful and he loved them, but he had no intention of ever putting anyone through the experience his friend Logan had just suffered. That had affected him more than he liked.

Chance had never actually seen such a serious injury up close; Logan had almost died. So much violence done to the human body as his friend lost control and plummeted down the icy ridges of the mountain they had been skiing, landing in a patch of trees. It had been one of the few things that had ever truly frightened Chance. Luckily, Logan hadn't hit any of the big pines or he would have died on the spot.

Chance had stayed with him through the helicopter ride out and had listened to Logan's earnest, painful request for what to tell his wife, Jillian, if he didn't make it. Chance had to call her and had picked her up at the airport, had taken her to the hospital.

Jill was one of the exceptions. A former Olympic athlete herself, she understood competition, drive and the need for adventure. She not only understood but encouraged Logan's need to do the things he did, whether it was extreme skiing or any of the other potentially life-threatening adventures he enjoyed.

Sometimes she even went with him.

But Chance still remembered how her legs had weakened, how she'd started to sink, as if her life had fallen out from under her when they had been let in to see Logan for the first time after surgery. Chance had done what he needed to, helping her stay strong for Logan, but it hadn't been easy.

It had shaken him to the core. He knew his family worried about him, and that was hard enough. It was the kind of thing that could get in your head, hold you back, make you hesitate. That was what could kill you.

Chance didn't want to ever hold back, and if he thought he could cause anyone the kind of pain that Jillian had suffered, he would have to quit living his adventurous lifestyle. And then, well, what would be the point?

Better to keep things loose. A woman in his bed but not in his life was what he often said.

Logan was going to be okay. He might never be able to extreme ski again, but he'd recover. He'd live to be with Jillian. Chance never told her what Logan had said on the plane. It hadn't been necessary, but it was in his head for good.

Now Chance needed to do something to stabilize that place inside him that had tilted off its axis. The accident had happened to Logan, not to him, right? He was fine. He was on a job doing work he loved. By the sound of it, the threat was local, and once they were in Mexico, it was likely that he would largely be on a babysitting vacation. Given the principal and the location, he wasn't complaining.

But they weren't there yet.

Breaking into the studio and getting by security had been a breeze. Locating and picking the lock on Ana's dressing room, again, easy. Why did they just let anyone in the door to see her? A stalker or anyone else could practically walk right in if they had just a few social-engineering or lock-picking skills.

Checking the status of her current security was his first job. Playing the role of the attacker, trying to see what barriers were in place.

Ana didn't like being held back, either, or caged in. She wanted to move around her life freely, without fear, and she resisted any real security they had wanted to implement. She still lived in her own apartment, drove her own car to work and refused to be limited in any way. Ana didn't think she needed a bodyguard; he'd decided this was an effective way to change her mind.

Chance could respect her need for freedom, except that now he would be the barrier, the enforcer of limits.

He was the one who stayed at her back and who would stand between her and anyone who wanted to harm her.

He'd been warned that she wasn't going to like it.

The firefighters dispersed, and Ana smoothed the front of her blouse as if readying for something. The motion brought his attention to her ample breasts, very delicious cleavage still peeking out from where she modestly buttoned up her red silk blouse.

She turned, facing him, and he waited, unmoving. Her hair was loose, black curls cascading everywhere, and his fingers itched for a handful.

Only in his imagination, he cautioned. Or maybe they could loosen the limits when they got south of the border and left the threats far behind.

"I'm sorry about that," she said with an apologetic smile. She had shadows under her eyes. She was tired. Worked hard, still smiled. Trying to charm him. Gone was the wildcat who had trapped an unwanted guest in her room, faced off, threatened him for possibly hurting her friend the security guard.

"For what?" he countered.

She shrugged prettily. She knew her effect on men. How many beautiful women didn't?

"For all of it. The thing in the room, keeping you here so late and making you wait while I signed things for the firemen," she said easily. "You could have gone. I'm heading home now. But I am glad to have had the chance to apologize for the chaos and for wasting your time."

"You're not wasting my time. I'm on the clock, bought and paid for," he said just as easily. "This is what I do. I watch you," he said and saw a flicker in her eyes. That had affected her.

Color infused her cheeks. Maybe it had affected her in a few different ways, he mused.

"Well, what I mean is, I don't need a bodyguard, and I'm really not interested. I appreciate you pointing out the holes in the security that you have, but honestly, the studio is overreacting. This simply isn't necessary."

"Yet you seemed to think it was necessary when you found me in your dressing room. I could have been anyone. I could have been *him*."

"I panicked, but I also got the firemen here, didn't I? I can take care of myself."

"The studio thinks differently."

"They're only worried about their bottom line, making sure everything is okay until we get the finale taped and I've chosen our winner. But seriously, the harassment isn't that big of a deal. I'm also leaving town the day after tomorrow, and that will make any protection unnecessary," she explained. "I doubt very much whoever is bothering me will follow me to Mexico."

Chance shrugged one shoulder. "Maybe, maybe not. We'll see."

Pretty, dark brown eyes fringed with thick lashes that were completely natural as far as he could tell, not cosmetic, narrowed.

"What do you mean, we'll see?" she demanded.

"We'll see if they follow you to Mexico. And if they do, I'll be there."

"You'll…what? No, you can't go to Mexico with me. Absolutely not."

"The studio has paid for my time for the next two weeks, until you return, and possibly after, to provide your protection. They have also paid for my ticket to Mexico, on your flight," he said, pulling the ticket from his pocket and showing it to her. "My seat is right next to yours, as you can see."

She actually tried to grab it away from him but wasn't fast enough.

"I refuse," she said, planting her hands on her hips, her eyes snapping. "This is ridiculous! I am going *home*. To my *family*. For the *holiday*. This is not the time nor place for this, this…intrusion. They have no right, and you have no right to thrust yourself in on my private time with my family," she spat angrily, stepping up close to him.

*Wow,* he thought, heat shooting through him. After this job was over, he had to have Ana Perez in his bed or anywhere else she'd have him. But for the moment, he kept his cool.

"Sorry, Ana, but apparently your contract says differently. Don't worry. I'm good at what I do, and parents tend to like me," he said cheekily, knowing it would annoy her. He liked watching her color rise and her eyes snap. Sexy as hell. "It'll be fun," he added just for kicks.

She looked as if she might hit him.

"You may be used to intimidating people or winning them over with that cocky charm," she said, clearly seething.

"Thanks," he interrupted. "Cocky charm. I like that."

She bit her lip as if holding back, and it just made him want to kiss her.

"Listen, I know they hired you, and you have a job to do, but this isn't going to happen," she said, changing tactics and appealing to reason, as much as her temper would allow. "How would I even explain you to my family? Have any of you thought of that?"

He pursed his lips, letting his eyes fall on hers. Her

mouth was drawn tight, and he felt the challenge of wanting to kiss it into softness.

"Well, they can't know who I am, that's rule number one. You can't let anyone know I'm your protection detail—that gives us the edge. So make something up. Tell them we're lovers," he suggested with a shrug.

Ana swallowed hard and took a deep breath that released in a frustrated growl as she turned away, striding back down the hall and into her dressing room, slamming the door behind her. Inside the room, Chance made out a litany of extremely colorful curses in a skillful blend of Mexican and English.

As she emerged, keys in hand, and headed for the exit, he waited a few seconds, giving her some space before he followed.

This *was* going to be fun.

## 2

ANA STEPPED INTO THE COZY entryway of the brownstone that she rented down in Brooklyn and made her way up the stairs and down the narrow hall to her apartment, letting herself in with a sigh of relief. Her landlady had decorated the place for the holidays, and the holly and poinsettias were still healthy and lovely, cheering her a bit as she passed them. She loved this place.

Closing the door, however, she stopped short. There was an envelope on the floor and it had Ana's name on it, but it was handwritten. Perhaps she had dropped it earlier? She tried to control the fear that was already choking her, but she knew she hadn't. She'd never seen this. Maybe her landlady had left it for her—but why on the floor?

Picking up the strange envelope, she opened it, and something fell out all over her hands, along with a piece of paper.

Ana's heartbeat raced as she stared down at the polished hardwood floor, her mind spinning as she focused and realized what had fallen out of the envelope—it looked like rose petals. Dried and black, they decorated her feet. Bending, she retrieved the paper that had fallen out with them.

Have a safe trip, Ana. I'll be waiting for you when you come back.

Ana shoved the note into her pocket with shaking hands, her thoughts momentarily drowned out by the liquid fear that blanked her mind.

He'd been in here. There was no space under the door to shove anything, so whoever had left this had to have been inside her apartment.

He could still be here.

She had to get out, call the police and have them check the place for her. Making her way back out to the stairs as quietly as she could, she rushed outside into the freezing-cold darkness. Frantically, she pulled her phone out of her pocket.

A firm hand stopped her from dialing, and Ana almost screamed as she realized someone was right there, right next to her, until she looked up.

Chance Berringer.

Everything inside of her seemed to melt in relief, and she forgot to be scared or agitated. She'd checked him out; he was indeed her bodyguard, and right now, that was okay with her.

"Hey, what happened? Talk to me, Ana," Chance said, supporting her with one strong arm as he directed her to his car.

"What are you doing here?" she had the presence of mind to ask, but answered her own question before he could. "You followed me home."

"That is my job. Now, tell me what scared you so much," he said, his eyes perceptive and hawklike.

If he had been impressive back at the studio, Chance was ten times more so inside the small, intimate space. He wasn't wearing cologne, but Ana could smell his soap, and she was close enough to study the strong line of his jaw and note the way the hair at the nape of his neck laid curled slightly against his skin. The muscles in his upper arms were impossible not to admire as he laid an arm along the back of the seat.

Swallowing hard, Ana quickly looked away.

"So what happened?" he asked smoothly.

"Just a note from my…fan," she said, trying to sound unconcerned.

"Where?"

"In my apartment. On the floor when I walked in. He had to have been there. He might still be there." She shoved the note at him.

Ana hated feeling weak, something she didn't experience too often, but fear had nearly paralyzed her. Very few people knew where she lived; she kept her private life as separate from work as she could. No one should have found her here.

Chance cursed under his breath. "Any previous indication he or she knew where you lived?"

Ana shook her head. "No. Everything so far was through the studio."

He read it quickly, and she watched his pursed lips draw into a tight, flat line. He didn't like what he saw.

Would she have to move? She dismissed the thought as soon as it rose in her mind. Drug gangs had terrorized her village in Mexico for years, trying to use it as a path to the coast, and never made her people back down. She certainly wasn't about to do so now because of some stalker fan who got their kicks out of trying to scare her.

"In Mexico, it won't be any problem—clearly he's not following me there. The note even indicates that," she said, returning to her first instinct that she didn't need his services. "And now that I am less panicked, I can see he's probably not still in my apartment, either. He just left this there."

Though maybe when she came back she wouldn't argue about having some protection until this was settled. And maybe she would stay with one of her friends for a while.

"Give me your keys," he said, and she did.

"What are you going to do?"

"You wait here, lock the doors and do not open them for anything. If there's trouble, hit the horn. I'll be right back down," he said, exiting the car.

Ana watched as one light after another was turned on in her apartment until the whole place was lit. Chance's tall silhouette moved slowly past some of the windows, stalking.

Checking.

Ana waited, as she was told. It was too late, and she was too tired and too relieved to have someone making sure her home was safe.

Minutes later, Chance came back down, opened the car door and ushered her out, beeping it to lock the car behind him.

"Everything's clear. I couldn't find any other signs of intrusion, though maybe you'll notice something. Good thing you were wearing gloves—maybe we'll find some prints on the letter or the rose petals. Those were pretty creepy. No wonder you freaked out," he said easily, making her feel less stupid about her fear as they headed up the stairs together.

"Thank you for checking the place out. I was calling the police to do just that," she said, taking her key from him.

"No need to give them more work to do. That's what I'm being paid the big bucks for," he said lightly with a smile as she opened the door.

She looked at him furtively from the door; the rose petals had all been picked up. He probably only did that to save them as evidence, but it still made her feel better.

"Thank you, Mr. Berringer. I'll be fine now. Good night," she said, starting to close the door.

"Call me Chance. If you need me, I'll be right downstairs," he said, turning away.

Ana paused. "Downstairs? Aren't you going home? I understand you followed me home to make sure I got here safely, and I appreciate it, but I'm fine now. Safe and sound," she said. "My landlady lives right below me, and I doubt whoever left this will be back."

Chance nodded. "You're probably right about that, but no, I'm not going home. I'm your bodyguard, and that's 24/7. No going home until the job is done. I checked out your building earlier, and the front entrance is the most viable entry point. The windows on the lower floor are barred, and the back door is hooked up to an alarm. Mostly likely your landlady inadvertently let in your stalker, or he picked the front lock. I'll talk to her in the morning."

"So you're going to stay in your car? All night?" Ana asked incredulously.

"It won't be the first time. Comes with the job. Let

me see your cell phone," he said, and Ana found herself handing it to him. "My number is the first one on your quick dial if you need me. 'Night," Chance said as he left.

She stood in the doorway for another stunned second and then shook her head.

"Well, if he wants to sit in his car all night, in the dead of winter, then fine," she said aloud to no one, closing the door. She hung her coat and tried to recapture the peace and happiness that she always felt when she came back here every night.

The apartment was small, not even the entire second floor of the building, but that appealed to her. She liked the cozy space with its freshly painted gold walls and bright hardwood floors. She had layered hand-loomed rugs from Mexico all through the apartment, had decorated it with as many things from the Yucatán as she could. Dense plants and large potted palms and ferns stood underneath warm lights and in front of the windows in every room, giving the apartment a lush, warm presence. Family pictures and art from a small gallery in Merida that she supported hung on the walls. Ana felt her muscles relax as the panic subsided, the threat gone.

She tried not to think about a stranger being in her home—two of them in one night, if she counted Chance Berringer. She surveyed the space carefully as she moved through it, checking to see if anything had been tampered with or touched. Nothing that she could tell. Somehow, that was even more disturbing. If not for the note, would she have even known someone had been here?

Changing into a soft nightgown and a matching robe, she poured a glass of wine and paused at the window, looking down at where Chance's car was still parked. Lights off, there was no exhaust. Had he shut the ignition off completely? How would he stay warm?

Ana stepped back from the window, closing the curtain. Not her problem. He was the one who insisted on camping out in front of her building, so it was his problem.

She grabbed a book she had been meandering through for several evenings before bed and shut off the lights in the rest of the apartment, heading to bed to read, finish her wine and hopefully to sleep.

She pulled the large quilt that her mother had made up over herself and settled in, comfortable and warm, and opened her book.

Still, minutes later, she found herself reading the same page. Her mind wouldn't adhere to the words, her eyes drifting to the window as she noticed through an opening in the curtain that snowflakes were falling; they danced in the light that streamed down from the nearest streetlamp.

It was supposed to be extremely cold tonight.

But Chance Berringer was a big boy. No doubt he had done this many times before. She didn't need to worry about him. Maybe he'd get cold enough to finally give up and go home.

Ana dropped the book with a frustrated sigh. No. She didn't know him well, but she was astute enough to know that men like Chance Berringer didn't give up on anything. He'd sit out there all night and freeze, but he'd stay and watch. Making sure she was safe.

She felt the weight of disapproval from her upbringing. Her parents would be ashamed of her lack of hospitality for someone who had helped her.

Ana knew she wouldn't be able to sleep unless she at least made the offer, and she did have a comfortable sofa. It wasn't much, but it was better than sitting out in his car on the street. She wrapped herself in her robe again and headed back downstairs. She'd offer Chance her sofa, and if he turned her down, then her obligation was fulfilled.

Somehow, she knew it wasn't going to be as easy as that.

HOT COFFEE AND EQUALLY HOT thoughts kept Chance awake, but they didn't mean he was comfortable as he shifted in his seat again. Every now and then he stretched his legs by getting out of the car and checking the perimeter of the building. This wasn't his first rodeo, and as he worked through the stash of chocolate and extra-strong coffee he'd brought along for the night, he couldn't help but think of Ana, upstairs, sleeping.

He'd followed the progression of lights on and off in her windows, until only one soft light stayed on. Her bedroom. It was still on. Had she fallen asleep that way, with the light on? Still afraid.

He didn't blame her. She was a strong, gutsy woman, but having a stranger in your house was enough to shake anyone up. Chance almost hoped that the creep came back so he could settle this here and now. He'd like nothing better than to end this for Ana.

Well, there might be a few things he'd like better. Like knowing what she wore to bed, if anything, and how firm her mattress was.

He'd had a peek when he'd checked out the apartment, and liked her sense of decor, obviously inspired by her home country. She loved strong colors, textures, and everything about her screamed *passion*.

The entertaining thoughts were simply a way to keep himself occupied while he watched and waited. Sipping his coffee, his tired brain suddenly perked awake and took notice as he saw another light come on and then one more in the hall. Two seconds later, Ana was standing in the doorway of the brownstone, waving to him.

Chance was out of the car and by her side in the blink of an eye, his eyes searching behind her.

"What's wrong? What happened?" he asked, standing close, protecting her with his own body, though he couldn't figure out what he was protecting her from.

She sighed. "I was just coming down to get you, to tell you to come in. I can't believe you're still out here. It's freezing!" she said, stepping back into the warmth of the hallway.

Chance looked at her, absorbing what she'd said. "You're okay?"

She nodded impatiently. "Yes, I'm fine, but close the door and come on up. You're letting all the cold in," she said and went to climb the stairs.

Chance's gaze honed in on slim calves and ankles exposed as she moved up the stairs, holding the flannel robe around her curvy form. His pulse had spiked from the adrenaline, and it wasn't settling down any as his eyes took in the nice curve of her behind.

He shook himself out of it, looking away, beeping his car lock and closing the door, as she'd instructed.

She was asking him upstairs.

Not a romantic invitation—in fact, she looked more irritated than anything—but Chance wasn't going to say no, anyway. Taking the steps two or three at a time, he was by her side as she opened the door.

It was considerably warmer inside, he had to admit. Even his jangling caffeine-and-sugar-fed nerves were settling once he stepped into the refuge of Ana's apartment.

"Thanks. This is a lot nicer than the car."

"The couch is yours. I'll get you some blankets and sheets. You know where the bathroom and the kitchen are from when you looked around earlier. You can use the bath out here. I have my own. Help yourself to anything you want," she said, her tone coolly polite, but as her eyes met his and locked on for a second, a flicker of heat betrayed her. She felt it, too.

Chance ignored it. This was difficult for her, he could tell. Her apartment had been invaded by some stranger, and her life was being invaded by, well, him. To take advantage of that, of her vulnerability, that wasn't just against his professional reputation—it wasn't his style. He was here to make her feel safe, and that was what he intended to do.

"Thank you, Ana," he said sincerely, hanging his coat neatly over the back of a chair. "I'll be fine. You get some sleep. Long day tomorrow."

The change in his tone seemed to throw her, and he wondered what she had expected. His eyes measured the generously cushioned sofa. It would be plenty comfortable for him, while allowing him to stay close and hear anything that happened throughout the apartment. Maybe he'd even sleep a little.

"Long day?"

"You have meetings and then your flight early the next morning."

She closed her eyes. "Of course, you know my schedule."

He shrugged. "Part of the job."

She nodded, pushing a hand through her hair and suddenly looking weary and a little fragile. "We'll talk about that tomorrow."

He wasn't going to argue, but set to pulling out a few blankets from the pile she'd stacked at the foot of the long sofa. "Good night, Ana."

Pausing, she returned the sentiment and walked quietly into her room.

Chance made the sofa up for something to do and even laid down on it, though he had no intention of sleeping, even if he could. He'd primed his body and mind for staying awake all night, and if the sugar and caffeine weren't enough, all he had to do was think about Ana only yards away, in bed.

Still, rest would get him through the next twenty-four to forty-eight hours until he could get Ana safely to Mexico.

Lying back into the soft blankets and pillows, his body remained tense, his mind alert. He closed his eyes, taking some smooth, relaxing breaths, and then opened them again. It was no use.

Sitting back up, he studied the room and got up to poke around a little. Several bookcases were jammed with volumes of fiction, nonfiction—a lot of travel writing—and what had to be hundreds of cookbooks. Including four written by Ana.

Chance loved food almost as much as he loved women. His extreme-sports lifestyle allowed him to eat pretty much anything he wanted, though he rarely cooked for himself. It wasn't at the top of his list of skills, for sure. Spotting a shelf of DVDs, he thought he might find something to watch and noticed several hand-labeled *Ana's Kitchen*. Ana's cooking show that she'd filmed herself. Some early college-age episodes and some later, from her network show.

Curious, Chance took one and put it in the DVD player, lowering the volume. He had to grin at the perky Mexican music that introduced the clearly amateur-filmed episode, but as soon as Ana appeared on the screen, he was rapt.

He had no idea what she was cooking, but he loved watching her do it. She was so young then, more re-laxed, though just as beautiful. She wore a crisp white shirt, a yellow apron and had a flower in her hair. Her friends from the dorm would pop into the kitchen and help her, and Ana practically burst with energy and spark as she cooked and explained step-by-step how to create what she was cooking in her small kitchen.

Chance studied her expressions, her movements, how she laughed freely with her friends. She was so much more open. Happier.

"What are you doing?"

The fact that her question made him jump proved how absorbed he was in his observations. She stood in the doorway, wrapped in the same flannel robe, her arms crossed in front of her. She looked tired, her eyes sleepy, hair mussed. No makeup.

Still sexy as hell.

"Couldn't sleep. Watching some of your old shows that I found in the bookcase. Is that okay?"

It hadn't occurred to him that she might not want anyone to see them—it had been a broadcast show, after all.

"It's fine," she said with a yawn. "I just heard sounds, and I didn't know what it was. I forgot you were here for a second. I'm not used to anyone being in the apartment at night. It startled me before I remembered."

"Sorry about that. I tried to keep it low," Chance said, watching her as she moved closer and sat with him, curling her feet up under her in that feminine way women did. He'd always liked that, how they could fold themselves up like cats, unfold like flowers.

He blinked at the TV, surprised by his own late-night poetry. Maybe Ana brought it out in him. There was something comforting and intimate about sitting with her like this on a sofa covered in blankets and pillows. He'd kept his jeans and T-shirt on, but it felt…homey.

"It's a great show," he said, following her gaze to the TV. She smiled to herself as she watched. "How many of these did you do?" he asked her.

"Two years in college, then one after, before I was picked up by the networks. Sixty-seven episodes in all. We didn't follow any particular plan. I just cooked a lot, and when my friends were free to film, we did. It was fun."

"And by the looks of it, you paid them with the results," he said. Every show ended with the group diving into whatever dish Ana had made.

"Pretty much. It wasn't about money. We didn't care about that, though the show gave us all our start, in a way. Alan, the guy who did the video, went on to be a cameraman on several popular TV shows, and Patty—that brunette right there—she's a writer now. They were the main ones in it with me, and others just joined in spontaneously."

"You were amazing on camera then, too. A natural," Chance said, and he meant it.

She shook her head. "I never imagined any of this would happen. I wanted to keep doing the show and the cookbooks."

"That's unusual," Chance said. "Most people want to be famous."

"A generation of cooks before us came up from family restaurants, small kitchens, and they knew food better than they knew anything else. I try to honor that knowledge on the new show as much as I can. Not everyone needs to have studied at Le Cordon Bleu or the Culinary Institutes. Some of the more creative chefs never have formal training, though it's not a bad thing to have. I just got very lucky."

"I'd say instead that you are just very, very good at what you do."

Ana switched her gaze from the TV to meet his. "Thank you. I think I am, though I'm always learning. I think if I spend my whole life doing this, I will never learn all there is to know about food. It's one of the things I love about it. The challenge. The simplest dish can be the hardest to perfect."

Chance watched her face light up as she talked about her craft, her profession. She really did love it.

"You miss it," he said. A statement, not a question. He could see it in her eyes.

She nodded. "Sometimes, yes."

He reached out to push back a stray curl that had fallen forward into her face. She sucked in a tiny, surprised breath as his fingers drifted over her cheek and the back of her ear—so soft—but she didn't pull back. It would be so easy to let his fingers slip into that mass of silky hair and draw her close, get tangled in the blankets and sheets together.

Instead, he dropped his hand, smiling slightly.

"Maybe we should try to sleep again," he said, taking a breath. "I'll turn this off now."

She stood, looking as disconcerted as he felt. Because what he'd done was out of line, or because she felt the same tug of desire?

"Yes, of course. Good night, again."

Without another look, Ana padded back to her bedroom, closing the door with a definite click. Chance could imagine a hundred other ways that moment could have ended, but this one was the right way. For now.

But if he had his way, when things were better, he might try to steal that kiss—or more—from Ana and see what happened. It was a thought that followed him into his dreams.

## 3

ANA SLIPPED INSIDE her dressing room and locked the door. She leaned back against it, letting out a sigh of relief.

Finally, alone.

She was exhausted from being up all night, then arguing with the studio executives about Chance accompanying her to Mexico, and everything in between. She'd excused herself from the current, deadly discussion that was going on back in the conference room. Everyone would assume she was just going to the ladies' room. Chance wouldn't follow, as it was only down the hall, and he had already secured the floor.

She had barely a few minutes to make her escape before they caught on.

She'd changed her flight online that morning and had scheduled a car to come get her; it should be waiting out back. Ready to take her to the airport and away from all of this craziness.

Ana wasn't the studio's property; she wasn't anyone's property. She ran her own life, her way. While it had been lucky to have Chance there the night before when she discovered the note in her apartment, he was *not* coming home with her.

Gathering up her things, Ana left the dressing room unnoticed and dashed for the emergency exit, where she would be in the car and on a jet heading south before they could figure out where she'd gone. She'd be home before nightfall.

Once she was on the plane, she would text to let them know that she was safe and bid them adios.

It had been snowing all morning, and she paused for a moment as the brisk air cooled her skin. Taking a deep breath and letting the stress go, she stared up at the steel-gray sky, soon to be replaced by the rich blue of her homeland. She couldn't wait.

The car was there, not twenty feet away, and she hurried to it, letting herself in and collapsing back into the luxurious seat as she closed her eyes.

"Let's go," she said and didn't bother opening her eyes as the car rolled forward, out onto the road.

The studio people would have a fit, but she could care less. What would they do? Fire her? Maybe they'd be doing her a favor. She'd been ready to scream every time one of them talked to her in their overly solicitous, pandering tone. They kept saying all they wanted was to keep her safe, when in reality, all they wanted was to protect the money she made for them. The more profitable the show became, the more control they tried to exert. When she was home, she could think about what she wanted to do next.

Her contract was up after this season. It had been a given that she would renew her contract. Plans were already in progress for the third season, but doubt flickered somewhere in the back of her mind. Sitting with Chance, watching her old show the night before, she wondered if she really could keep doing this. But what else would she do?

Go back to producing a cooking show of her own? Write books? Open a restaurant?

Those options had all crossed her mind, and somewhere, in the back of the fog of ambition, perhaps, someday, a man. A husband. Children.

Ana shook her head. She did regret ditching Chance, which would no doubt make him look incompetent and earn him censure from the studio. He would certainly be fired, and that bothered her deeply. But it couldn't be helped. He'd be fine, she was sure. He was good at his job, and she couldn't be the first client to refuse protection.

Ana hated doing this to him, but it was the position she had been put in. She'd find a way to apologize later. Maybe if they had met some other way, some other time, she might have enjoyed knowing him. When he'd touched her, the warmth from his hands had seeped down to her bones, setting off an answering response in her blood. It had been a while since that had happened. If he had been anyone else, maybe she would have invited him back to her bed last night.

A nice thought. Too late now.

Sighing again, Ana opened her eyes and frowned as she took in the route.

"This is not the way to the airport," she said, sitting upright in alarm.

No response from the driver. Fear clenched in her belly as she leaned forward.

"Where are we going? I demand you take me to the airport," she said, finding her phone. "I'm calling the police," she told the man driving the car and started to dial.

"No need for that, Ana. I've got you covered."

The voice was all too familiar, and as he readjusted the rearview mirror and took off the driver's cap, Ana's eyes widened as they met Chance's familiar green ones.

"How could you—" she sputtered.

"I paired my cell phone to yours last night when I gave you my number. I watched as you changed your plans this morning. Clever. You might want to let them know you're okay before they call out the troops, though," he said easily, returning his attention to the road.

"Where are we going? This isn't the way to the airport."

"No, it's not. It wasn't a bad idea to change your flight, actually, seeing as someone was in your apartment, and your flight schedule was on your desk. But I have an even better plan. It'll be fine. You'll enjoy it. Trust me," he said and hit the gas, speeding them down the highway.

Ana was shaking with so much fury, frustration and so many other emotions that she couldn't name that words deserted her, as did her hope of going home alone and leaving all of this behind for a few weeks. How could she truly leave, let it all go, with a bodyguard dogging her every step? And how was she going to explain him to her mother? Her family?

Her fiancé?

She watched sullenly as they turned down a dirt road that led to a small airport and pulled into a hangar where a man waited for them, obviously having been preparing the small turboprop plane that he was standing beside. A plane painted in gray cammo.

Chance shot her a look. "Wait here."

He got out of the car and, this time, opened the back,

grabbing her bags and tossing them to the other man. Ana got out of the car and followed.

"Thanks, Don, for getting her ready on such short notice," Chance said to the other man.

"No problem, Chance. I was out here doing some other work already. Glad to help," he said with a smile aimed at Ana.

Chance stepped between them, blocking Don's view and not bothering to introduce her. Ana stepped around him, holding out her hand, starting to say hello.

Chance took her elbow and turned her away, saying something else to Don over his shoulder as they walked out.

"What is the matter with you? That was rude!" she said, pulling her elbow away.

"I told you to stay in the car, first off. Don is trustworthy, but the fewer people who know who you are or that you were even here, the better."

Ana took a deep breath, trying to hold her temper. Maybe she could reason with him.

"Cut the Jason Bourne act. Don't you think this is taking things a little too far? I doubt my stalker has the kind of reach or ambition to follow me home. I'll be fine. Please, just take me to the airport and leave me be."

Chance turned on her, his light green eyes burning into hers. He was dead serious, she could see.

"You'd be surprised what determined people are willing to do when they want something badly enough. Take my word for it. And don't worry about being rude. Don isn't offended. He knows the score."

"Is he the pilot?"

Chance smiled. They approached the tarmac as the engine of the small plane came to life behind them.

Don rolled it out of the hangar, and they watched as it came to a stop.

"No. I am. It's my plane. I flew it up here last night from Philly."

Ana saw her hopes of visiting in Mexico alone vanish. As the engines of the plane became too loud for them to say anything, Ana growled in frustration, the sound lost in the noise. It looked as if she was stuck with Chance Berringer, whether she liked it or not.

CHANCE HAD TO ADMIT THAT he was a little gleeful at being able to take the King Air—a plane that he had refurbished completely on his own—for a long flight. He hadn't had the chance to do that in a while. Taking Ana to Mexico was an added perk to the job, and he could even bill the production company for the expense. Sweet.

Being cozied into the little space with Ana for several hours wasn't any hardship, either, even if she was a bit high maintenance.

Chance could handle that. He loved things that were fast, dangerous and presented a challenge. Sliding a look to where Ana's skirt had brushed up higher on her thigh, he knew she wouldn't disappoint on any of those points.

But she was also in trouble, whether she wanted to admit it or not. It wasn't unusual for people to rail against protection. No one wanted their privacy invaded to the degree that bodyguards often had to insert themselves into a person's life. And the loss of control was harder for some to handle than others. Chance could relate—he didn't like losing control of a situation, either, and for that reason, he didn't plan to let anything happen to Ana Perez.

And if she wasn't just flat-out one of the most beautiful women he'd ever seen, she was also fascinating. He'd read and researched her background well into the night and had never met anyone quite like her.

Ana had grown up in the small village of Hatsutsil, just outside of the larger Yucatán city of Mérida. Chance spoke decent Spanish, having spent four years in high school studying and several vacations in Central America, but he didn't know much about the Mayan people.

"So do you speak Mayan at home?" he asked as he checked the controls and did his preflight routine. It would be a long flight if they wouldn't speak to each other.

"There is no such thing," she said, arms crossed in front of her and her eyes straight ahead. Still pissed.

"What do you mean?"

She frowned but then answered his question. "Most of what my family speaks is called Yucatec Maya, one version of Mayan, but largely they also speak Spanish and most are proficient to some degree in English."

"I thought Maya was how the group of people is referred to? The language, as well?"

"Mayan is a class of languages—like Italian and Spanish are Romance languages. There are many variations within Mayan. Maya is how we refer to our people. You won't have any trouble finding that most people speak and understand English."

Chance nodded, silent as he signaled Don and then started down the runway.

"Good to know. Anything else I should know about the people or the area so that I don't put my foot in my mouth?" he asked in Spanish this time.

She looked at him, seeming surprised at the question.

"You will be fine. And you may not be there long, after all."

"We'll see," he said with a smile, enjoying the thrill as the small plane lifted into the bleak winter sky and he banked southwest, taking them away from New York.

What he also knew from her file was that she had funneled most of her earnings back into the village, building schools, security and small businesses. She'd made her hometown stronger and less of a target for crime, including that which resulted from local drug wars.

Ana was mistaken if she thought she would shake him once they were down in Mexico, if for no other reason than he had discovered her name mentioned twice in recent chatter about possible kidnappings. Of course they knew she was coming home, and it wasn't unusual for celebrities and people who had money to become targets for a number of groups in that part of the world.

"You may be mistaken about being in danger in Mexico," he said, floating the idea for her consideration. "There have been some rumors about possible kidnappings. I have a friend in the FBI who gave me a heads-up."

To Chance's surprise, Ana laughed.

"That's funny?"

"Not funny, just not unusual. There are always threats for kidnapping. And worse. I don't pay any attention to that," she said dismissively.

"You're not worried?"

She looked him directly in the eye. "No. We grew up with the drug runners terrorizing our village. We're near the coast. It's an easy delivery route. Once you've lived with that, it's hard to be worried about rumors.

If there is any real threat, the police in our village will handle it. I'm perfectly safe there."

She wasn't just putting on a brave facade. Ana really had no fear, and that made her even more attractive to him.

She wasn't married, and there weren't any current boyfriends. They would have been part of her profile. Not interested in men?

No. He'd seen the heat in her eyes a few times when he'd touched her. She felt it, too.

As they reached the right altitude and leveled off, he set the autopilot and leaned back, relaxing in his seat.

"So who do you think could be doing this? A fan? Or maybe someone closer?" he asked, deciding that this was as good a time as any to talk about who was harassing her.

"It's clearly a fan."

"Or perhaps someone trying to appear like a fan."

"What do you mean?" Ana asked, sitting up, her eyes sharp.

"I talked to your landlady, and she said she didn't let anyone into your apartment yesterday. She was very clear on the issue. There was also no forced entry."

"So you suspect...who?"

"Anyone who might've had access to your keys during the day. Anyone who could have grabbed them and ducked out while you were too busy to notice or who knows your schedule. When you are and are not home."

Ana started to say something, then dropped back into her seat again, silent.

"Anyone on the show have it in for you?" he asked.

She barked a slight laugh that was not humorous. "Every contestant that hasn't won. So many. Who knows?"

"That bad?"

"It can be. I make a decision that changes people's futures, makes their dream come true. When those dreams are ruined, people can be very…upset."

He nodded. "Anyone in particular? Someone who might want to give you a hard time or throw you off your game?"

"Nothing throws me off my game," she stated, making him smile. "There is Lionel. He's been a problem. I can't imagine he would have done anything like this, though."

"Tell me about him."

"He's your typical rich guy who has bought his way through life, including onto the show. He has some talent in the kitchen, but I would never choose him to win, and he knows it."

"Why?"

"He's not *that* good, and he's a pain in the backside. He's asked me out no fewer than eight times so far, and I finally told him that if he didn't stop, I'd disqualify him from the show immediately—his contract included clauses that held him to strict behavioral guidelines, including no bribing or influencing of the show's judge or crew."

"That couldn't have gone over well."

"Lionel seemed to think he was above all of it. Coming on to me was his way of letting me know he had no respect for me. His father put some background pressure on my producer through the network. I told them all to go to hell."

"Good for you. What happened?"

"I tried to have him removed from the show after his last display, and his father's blatant manipulation, which is against the rules. The studio promised to 'talk' to him, but they wouldn't go along with tossing him out. Clearly, his father has some real pull with the studio execs. Lionel wasn't happy."

Chance whistled between his teeth. "Sounds like a good suspect."

"I guess. But death threats? Breaking into my apartment? Somehow I don't see him getting his hands dirty like that."

"He could always pay someone to do it for him."

Ana sat back, considering. "I never suspected it could be someone inside. We all have disagreements, but we work together. We may not be friends, but we are a team."

Chance took in her face, the tired shadows beneath her eyes. None of this was easy.

"There's room in the back if you'd like to go stretch out, relax. It's not superluxurious, but you can read or take a nap," he said congenially.

"Thank you. That would be nice," she said, clearly eager to escape as she released her belt.

Chance comforted himself that he'd have plenty of time with her once they landed. Maybe he could find a way to convince her that he wasn't the enemy. And in the meantime, he could send a message to Garrett to check out this Lionel guy and maybe put a tail on him. If he was that determined and that wealthy, he could have the reach to get to Ana anywhere.

Chance was caught in thought as Ana stood, bracing herself as she turned to squeeze out of the tight space between them. Just then, some turbulence shook the plane and tipped just enough to throw her off balance.

With a solid *oomph,* Ana landed right in Chance's lap.

Chance's mind blanked and his body reacted to her

scent and the soft curve of her ass pressing into his lap. Her fingers grabbed his shoulder to steady herself as she wiggled forward, trying to pull herself back upright. Her skirt had ridden up to new heights, exposing a delectable view of smooth upper thigh that made Chance ache to know what was hidden just a few inches higher. Her wiggling against him wasn't helping.

"I'm so sorry," she said on a breath, her face mere inches from his. "Clumsy."

"Not your fault. Turbulence," he said, sounding a bit hoarse.

Her lips looked delicious. Big brown eyes widened as Ana watched him watch her, and it was all Chance could do not to pull her in closer and have a taste.

He was hard, and he knew she felt his response to her as warmth infused her cheeks. He wanted her, but it was up to him to stop this.

"I could come back with you, entertain you for the rest of the flight," he said with a naughty grin.

It did the trick. The pink in her cheeks turned red and her eyes snapped. Her fingers dug in as she arched out of his lap, taking all of that luscious softness away.

Glaring down at him, her chin tipped up. "I don't think so," she muttered, straightening her skirt and her spine.

Man, she was gorgeous.

Chance smiled at her. "If you change your mind, just say so."

With a small infuriated sound, Ana shot him one more look and headed to the back of the plane, where Chance was fairly sure she would stay until they landed.

Unfortunate, but just as well. He wanted her, bad. And with her safety in the balance, it was better if she was angry at him and kept her distance, or he might just throw caution to the wind, as he had a habit of doing.

But it still sucked. Taking the high road meant a long, lonely and uncomfortable ride to Mexico, that was for sure.

# 4

ANA TRIED READING, BUT FELL asleep instead, stretched across two of the not-very-comfortable seats. She was so exhausted that comfort hardly mattered. Sinking in and out of a restless slumber, her dreams kept returning to the moment in the cockpit.

Chance had looked at her mouth as if he was about to kiss her. She could still feel the strength of his shoulder under her hand, his heat as he'd hardened beneath her. In her dreams, she didn't struggle her way out of the seat and run away.

Instead, Chance was nuzzling her neck, his hand easing the material of her blouse away from her shoulder. Fingers ran lightly along her collarbone, making her shiver. She said his name, needing more. She wanted his mouth to touch every part of her....

Just as things were getting good, something jostled her quite violently and her eyes flew open. Her own hand lay in a very compromising position on her chest, and if anyone had been watching, there would have been no mistake about the dream she'd been having.

Luckily, she was still alone in the back of the plane

and thanked the bit of turbulence for shaking her out of what could have been even more embarrassing if the dream had gone any further.

Straightening up, she smoothed her clothes and looked at her watch, resetting it for the time-zone difference, which was only an hour earlier. Hatsutsil was in the central time zone, to many people's surprise. It was nice not to have to worry about jet lag when she visited.

They were about an hour away from landing, she presumed as she made her way up to the cockpit. The plane had offered a surprisingly smooth ride, except for bits of turbulence that couldn't be avoided. Now that she was a bit rested and closer to home, she was more excited, as well. Ana didn't want to miss seeing her homeland as they approached it; they were still over water at the moment.

"Hi, mind if I join you?" she asked Chance from the doorway, offering a smile and trying to be pleasant. She also tried to ignore the flicker of desire that kindled deep inside when he looked up at her, offering a slight smile in return.

"Help yourself," he said, turning back to tinker with the controls, a book turned over in his lap.

She made her way, more carefully this time, into the copilot's seat, belting in.

"Sorry about the turbulence. Hit an air pocket," he said, reaching forward to adjust something.

"It's fine. I did get some rest. I feel much better and I'm excited to be so close to home," she said.

"Glad you slept. Makes the time go faster. It's been a pretty boring ride, which is a good thing, mostly," he said with a grin. "No one needs adventure when we're this far up."

In spite of his smile, Ana suddenly felt a pang of

guilt. He looked tired. Still sharp and focused, but he had to have gone without even more sleep than she had in the past forty-eight hours. She could have at least sat up here and kept him company, she chastised herself with a sigh.

Well, she was here now.

"When did you learn to fly?"

"I started when I was fourteen. I pestered my parents for lessons for two years before that."

"Fourteen!"

"Well, just taking lessons. Studying up. You can't solo until sixteen or officially be a pilot until seventeen. I had to work to pay for the lessons and the flight time, so I didn't actually become a pilot in the official sense until I was nineteen."

"And you have your own plane?"

"I won it," he said with a naughty grin that made her heart flip.

"That sounds like a good story."

"Nah. Just a bet that the other guy lost. He was supposed to shave his head if he lost, but he refused and offered me his junker plane instead. I snapped it up."

"This is hardly a junker."

"It was when I got it. Took me five years on and off to rebuild and refurbish it. I live in a small apartment that I rarely see and dumped most of my extra cash into the plane. And it was worth every cent," Chance added, and she could hear the pride in his voice.

Ana couldn't help but admire his determination and skill. It took both intelligence and dedication to take on such a task.

"Clearly, when you want something, you don't give up," she said with a chuckle.

The smile he sent her next was knee-melting.

"Yeah, that's pretty much true."

Flashes of her erotic dream popped into her mind, and Ana was suddenly flustered, as if he could see them, too. She straightened up in her seat to look out the window. In the distance, the lush green landscape of the Yucatán Peninsula stretched before them. The sight loosened the tension that had become so commonplace in her daily life that she almost forgot it was there. But now her heart warmed, her entire frame relaxing.

Home.

"I've never see it quite like this," she whispered, unable to take her eyes away from the view.

"Want to take her in?" Chance said, and Ana blinked, looking back in his direction.

"What?"

"Would you like to fly?"

Ana was taken aback for a second, and then the excitement rose. She couldn't say no.

"I would love to," she said. "How?"

"Pull your seat up a bit," he said and switched some things on the panel in front of him before leaning over close to her.

"Here, hold the yoke—it's just like the wheel on a car, sort of, except you go up and down instead of forward and reverse."

Ana took hold of the yoke and focused hard, excitement grabbing her. She couldn't believe she was going to actually fly a plane!

"This is your horizon. You want to keep it level. Since we'll be landing soon, you need to bring us down a little."

She nodded and tried to focus on the instrument panel as Chance leaned close, covering her hands with his.

"Let me help you get the feel of it. See, like this… It doesn't take much," he instructed and applied a firm pressure forward that started pointing the plane downward, but smoothly and at a gentle slope.

Ana could feel the power of the plane at her fingertips, and that of the man next to her, as well. The heat of Chance's body seeped into hers as his shoulder pressed against her.

"Now, you try it. Take us back up a bit, then down again," he said, settling back in his seat. "Don't worry. The sky is open. Just go when you're ready, take it slow."

His tone and his words hit her as particularly sensual, but Ana focused on the task, pulling the yoke gently back. That took them up a few hundred feet, and she leveled off, thrilled to have done it so easily. Then, after an encouraging smile from Chance, she took them back down to the previous level.

"This is wonderful!" she exclaimed, looking at him with unabashed excitement. "I've never minded flying, as a passenger, but this is an entirely different feeling."

Chance grinned widely, nodded. "It's like you're part of the sky," he said. "We're landing in about fifteen minutes. You want to try it?"

Ana bit her lip. "I think I'll leave that in your hands. But…I wouldn't mind a lesson or two, if you have time while we're here."

"I think that could be arranged," he said, his eyes warm as they met hers. "I knew you were an adventurous spirit," he said.

"Really? How could you?"

"You don't hold back. You have that way about you. Like this—I asked you if you wanted to fly, and you lit up and jumped right in. I like that," he said.

Ana tried not to show how pleased she was by his words. She didn't want, or need, any man's approval, but his words filled her with pleasure nonetheless. She wondered what other adventures, and what other pleasures, Chance Berringer could offer.

"My childhood was, in some ways, very traditional, but the Maya, and my family, never believed in holding children back. We were all allowed to explore the jungles, warned of the dangers, but allowed to find our own adventures from the time we were small."

"I read in your file that you have a sister. Are you close?"

"We always were, but sadly, I don't see her very often now. She studied to be a nurse and then started a local nonprofit that helps small villages build clinics for their people."

"That's pretty admirable," Chance said. "What's her name?"

"Lucia. She is a few years older than me." Ana sighed, taking a moment to follow Chance's instructions to bank the plane slightly left—lurching a bit, making them both laugh—and then leveling out even lower. The expanse of blue water shortened as the jungles appeared before them. They would head inland to the airport, over the treetops.

Ana thought that as soon as they were over land she would hand over the controls to Chance.

"She was always helping someone or bringing home strays. Lucia, I mean. Always so focused. I admire her and wish I was more like her."

"What do you mean? You're hardly a slacker."

Ana smiled. "I work hard, and I try to do what I can, but I often wonder how much meaning my work has in the world. Lucia helps to save lives. I...cook. And yell at people on television," she said with a rueful laugh.

"Hardly that. Your work has really helped your village and many others in Mexico. It was also in your file, but it's been in the news, in your interviews. Though I suppose I know what you mean. My brothers are all pretty accomplished, and now they are all getting married, moving on with their lives."

"And you are not?" Ana asked, curious.

"I don't want to," Chance answered with a grin. "I like my life as it is and make no apologies for that."

Ana understood. She lived the same way.

"I think maybe you should take the controls now," Ana said as the trees spread out below them. She knew from what she'd heard how complicated flying over the jungles could be, with the heat that rose up, the sudden storms. But she felt safe with Chance flying, watching him adjust the controls and altitude effortlessly, as if he were part of the plane itself. While he was completely absorbed in what he was doing, talking to the airport, she was free to study him.

He had great hands.

She wanted to know what they would feel like on her skin, for real, not in her dreams. Ana thought that was a very real possibility.

Perhaps...once she had cleared up her engagement to Marco, among other things, she and Chance could explore their options.

The possibility distracted her for the rest of the trip.

CHANCE LANDED IN MEXICO a much more hopeful man than he had been back in the States. Here, the sun was shining, the breeze was warm. There was friendly chatter and other pleasant sounds everywhere around them as they made their way through the airport.

He had barely held back from hauling Ana into his arms and kissing the life out of her when she had accepted his invitation to fly the plane. She'd been so... excited. Her eyes had sparkled with adventure, the air crackling between them. He'd never experienced anything quite like it with any woman.

He'd actually never taken a woman up in his plane before, let alone offered to let them fly it. While taking Ana in the plane had been a necessity of protecting her, offering to let her fly had been spontaneous. A test of sorts, perhaps.

Most of the women he knew were not terribly adventurous out of the bedroom, and that had always been fine with him. But his mind went back to Logan and Jill, how his friends were both extreme athletes and how that connected them.

Chance had met women who were adventurers in their own right, and dated a few, but he'd never felt that *click* until that moment with Ana—who was a chef, not an extreme athlete, but whom he believed would be up to just about anything he suggested. His former enthusiasm about the trip, about being here with Ana, returned as he signed the paperwork to store his plane while he was in Mexico. With that done he left the airport office to find Ana.

She had been sitting right outside when he'd gone in.

Now she was gone.

Spying the woman's bathroom across the way, he went over and stood outside, catching a young woman who walked out.

"Hey, was there a woman in there, Mexican, yellow blouse and grey skirt, blue bags?"

The young lady looked wary at first and then smiled with a little flirty nod of her head. "No, señor. There was no one in there but me, but if you are looking for someone…"

Chance grimaced and shook his head. "No, thanks, though," he said, hurriedly entering the lavatory to make sure that she was telling the truth. Checking each stall and a changing room in the back, he cursed again as he found them all empty.

Turning to leave, two older women stood in the doorway and watched him, horrified.

Chance muttered a partial apology in Spanish and pushed past them, intent on finding Ana. He'd never lost a client before, in the literal or figurative sense, and panic threatened to choke out clear thought. Where could she have gone?

Or had she been taken?

Chance returned back to the spot where she'd been sitting, and looked at the area from her perspective. Directly across the room was a pay-phone station; anyone could have hidden there, watching them.

There was a travel agency and a car-rental desk next to the phone station. Someone had to have seen her. Chance approached the clerks, trying to maintain his cool. With armed police on patrol, the last thing he wanted to do was look agitated.

"Excuse me," he said to an older woman who sat at the travel-agency desk. "But I seem to have misplaced my girlfriend," he offered in Spanish with what he hoped was a charming, and not desperate, grin.

*"¿Su novia?"*

"Yes, she was sitting right there, waiting for me, but now I can't seem to find her. Did you happen to notice where she might have gone?" Chance asked, describing Ana the best he could.

The woman frowned, and then her face lightened with realization.

*"Sí, sí,"* she agreed as she told Chance that she'd seen a woman sitting there, who had been approached by a man and had left with him.

"Did he force her? Was she taken?" Chance asked, lowering his voice and trying to remain calm.

"No." The woman shook her head, adding that the man was very handsome and Ana had seemed happy to see him and had gone willingly.

Chance's despair must have been evident on his face as the woman patted his arm and rattled something off in Spanish about how it happened to the best of men.

Chance thanked her briefly and walked back to the middle of the aisle. Airline passengers, police, workers milled around him, going about their business as he tried to decide what to do.

Why would Ana leave without telling him? What if she had been under duress?

It was the only explanation. She may not like having a bodyguard, and she had tried to give him the slip that morning, but he couldn't imagine she would do it again.

Ana had been kidnapped. He'd known it was a possibility, but he hadn't expected it here, right under his nose.

Chance opened his phone, calling his brother.

"Garrett?"

"Yeah? You on the ground?"

"I am, yeah. Easy flight, but I lost Ana."

"Excuse me?"

"I was doing the paperwork to store the plane while I'm here. She was sitting right there, not six feet away from me, but when I turned around, she was gone. A travel clerk said that she saw Ana leave with a handsome man, likely Mexican, maybe local, in casual clothes. The clerk said she looked happy to see the man, but he must have had a gun on her or was telling her to cooperate."

"Shit, Chance, really? You lost our client?" Garrett said, cursing again, and Chance winced. He was good at his job, but somehow, when he did mess up, even a little, he felt about five years old. Always the irresponsible baby brother.

But he couldn't focus on that; time was of the essence if they were going to find Ana. He'd broken a cardinal rule and let her out of his sight. He'd dropped his guard, and this was the price. Stupid.

"Any ideas how to proceed?" he asked, his self-disgust clear in his tone.

"I have a friend in the American embassy down there. He might be able to tell me what he's hearing regarding any kidnappings and if any news or ransom demands are being made. You should go to her town, to her family, and see if they can help. They might have local contacts who might know something."

Chance breathed for the first time in the past twenty minutes, nodding. "On it. Thanks, Gar."

"Don't beat yourself, up, bud. It happens to the best of us. Let's just find her," Garrett said, and Chance appreciated the support, though nothing would make him feel better until he found Ana and knew that she was safe.

"Thanks. I'll call when I know something. You, too."

"Definitely."

Chance went to the rental desk and was in a Jeep fifteen minutes later, finding his way to Hatsutsil, about fifty miles from the airport. Luckily most of the distance was highway, though the past fifteen miles or so was back roads into some coastal jungle that would have been awesomely gorgeous if he had noticed it at all.

A wooden sign announced that he had entered the small village, and Chance pulled to the side, scattering a bunch of chickens that had congregated by the side of the road. Hearing laughter, Chance looked up to see a group of young girls, teenagers, standing together on the porch of a small business, a grocery by the looks of it, watching him. When he made eye contact with one of them, more giggles.

Chance was hard-pressed not to smile back at the charming group, though their dark hair and pretty eyes made him think of how pretty Ana must have been at their age, and how they all would be beauties like her one day. Thinking about Ana at the hands of some kidnapper made something twist in his chest, and he waved the girls over, hoping they could help.

They shook their heads no, however, apparently versed in the ways of strangers, and knowing better. Chance understood, and turned the gas off, getting out of the Jeep and walking up to them, instead, keeping a distance that would make them feel safe.

*"Olá. Me llamo Chance,"* he said with a smile. They watched with big eyes and said shy hellos back.

"I'm looking for the family of Ana Perez. I am a friend from the States," he added, showing them a picture of Ana that had them nodding. One of the older girls, maybe sixteen, came forward.

"You know Ana?"

"Yes. We flew down here together, but then we got separated at the airport. I need to talk to her family, to make sure she's okay. Can you tell me where to find them?"

Chance's Spanish might be a tad rusty, but it was coming back to him, and the girl nodded, apparently deciding he could be trusted.

Minutes later, he was pulling up in front of a lovely adobe home, gardens gracing almost every corner along the stone-covered drive that led to the house.

Getting out, Chance stopped before reaching the door, unsure how he was going to explain to Ana's family that he had been in charge of protecting her and yet had allowed her to be kidnapped. That wouldn't earn him any points, for sure.

He knew from the file that Ana's father had passed away several years before and her mother lived here with one of Ana's aunts and a few cousins. Lucia, Ana's sister, as she had mentioned, was traveling a lot. Chance had known that from her file, but enjoyed hearing her talk about her family; clearly, they were close.

He knocked a few times. Maybe no one was home? The heat of the afternoon was getting thick, and he swatted at a bug that was trying to bite.

The door opened just as he cursed and swatted at the thing again, and he found himself looking at a man about his own age, who was watching him questioningly.

"May I help you?" he asked in softly accented English. The guy was built and looked like a Latino movie star in his beige cargo pants and black shirt. Work boots showed dirt and scuffing—one of Ana's cousins maybe?

"My name is Chance, Chance Berringer. I'm a friend of Ana Perez's from the States. We flew down here together, but I'm afraid I have bad news," Chance said. "I was at the airport with Ana, and she disappeared.

I think she may have been kidnapped," Chance said, waiting on the other man's reaction.

He smiled, shaking his head.

"Ana is safe. She has not been kidnapped."

Chance's eyebrows lifted. "I don't mean to argue, but—"

"Ana is here," he said simply and turned to call her name.

To say Chance was surprised was an understatement, and he was even more so when Ana appeared in the door. Only a slight flicker in her eyes showed that she was surprised to see him.

What did she think he would do? Just leave when he found her gone? Anger welled inside him.

"Ana? How come you left and you didn't let me know? My brother is in contact with the Mexican authorities, and I've been crazed thinking you were taken. What the hell is going on?"

Chance had stepped forward, his anger apparent, and the other man stepped forward, as well, blocking Ana from Chance's view. In the mood he was in right now, Chance was ready for anything, including a fight, and he met the man's eyes.

"Move."

"I don't think so, Mr. Berringer."

"I *will* move you, so—"

"You can try, *gringo*," the man said with equal derision and stubbornness. "But you will apologize to Ana for speaking to her like you did, and then you will leave."

"Yeah? And who are you?"

The man puffed up, never blinking. "I am Marco Espinoza, Ana's intended."

"Intended? Intended to what?"

Ana pushed forward, squeezing past Marco and meeting Chance's eyes, though not completely.

"Marco, stop. Chance is just doing his... He's a friend, like he said, and I was...rude. I left without thinking. I meant to call on the way but got caught up in conversation," Ana said. She was covering up. She smiled at him a little too brightly.

"Chance, I'm sorry. I just... Well, I can explain later. This is Marco Espinoza, my, um, fiancé."

Chance thought he couldn't be surprised one more time that day, but as he stared at her, and then back at Marco, he was wrong.

## 5

"I DON'T BLAME YOU for being angry," Ana said, biting her lip so hard it hurt. "I panicked. I didn't expect to see Marco, and when he showed up, I just…"

"Left? Nice one," he said, clearly disgusted. He faced the house, away from her.

Ana threw her arms up in the air as she and Chance talked alone in the garden behind her family home. Everything was in bloom, the flowers bursting with color around them, and there was a cool breeze in the shade of the large banyan and palm trees.

None of it soothed her as she took in the tension in Chance's shoulders and back, and the look in his eyes when she'd told him who Marco was—disappointment?

She felt ashamed of herself for handling it all so badly. No doubt Marco was wondering what was going on, as well. She'd told him to go and that everything was fine. Ana was having a harder time convincing herself of that. She'd wanted to avoid all of this, to handle it quietly and on the sidelines, but now it had blown up in her face.

Luckily, her mother was out shopping, and no one else was home yet from the workday.

"How could you be surprised? You called him. Your fiancé," Chance said.

"I called my aunt to let her know I was coming and that I was safe. I didn't ask them to send Marco. He just showed up. They must have sent him after I got off the phone."

Chance rotated his neck to loosen tension, grimacing as he looked up at the tall trees around them. Then, finally, he looked at her. His gaze was still accusatory.

"How could you not expect your fiancé to pick you up at the airport? Why aren't you wearing a ring, and why isn't there anything about this in your file?"

Ana blinked. "How detailed is this file you've mentioned? Apparently you don't know everything about my life, which is a comfort," she spat.

"We have client files on everyone we protect. Your studio presented us with a lot of it, and then we did some background checks and other research on our own. It's routine. And there was nothing in there about a fiancé."

"You have no right to have intruded in my life that way," she said hotly, her cheeks warm from more than the late-afternoon temperature.

"I had every right. It helps me keep you safe. You had no right to just take off without a word."

"I can do what I like. You are *not* my keeper," she argued back, digging in. He was infuriating!

"I guess not. That job would apparently be Marco's," Chance said. "But as it turns out, I'm the one being paid to do it, and I'm the one who will be held responsible if something happens to you. I thought we were clear on that."

"I told you I never wanted a bodyguard," she said.

"You did, but we don't always get what we want," he retorted, and Ana blinked as she heard more disappointment in his tone.

Chance crossed the distance between them, standing close.

"I don't like being lied to, Ana, and I really don't like being made to look foolish or incompetent, and that's what happened because of your silly stunt today."

Ana caught her breath. He was a chameleon, changing from moment to moment. At once, he was disarming and easygoing, or intense and focused. Now he was very, very angry. She could feel it radiating off of him, though not in a threatening way. He hadn't been angry about her trying to sneak off the first time, but this time was different. If anything, it created conflicting urges inside of her. She wanted to soothe him, and simultaneously felt desire spike, her own passionate nature sparked by his.

"Why do you care so much? Why does this matter so much to you?" she asked, unsure what else to say.

"I have a job to do, and I take pride in that. What I do reflects on all of my brothers and our business. I had to call them and confess that I'd messed up, and then I had to call them back to let them know I'd only been duped," he said, shoving his hands in his pockets and turning away from her again. "I don't know which is worse."

Ana's anger and self-righteousness dissolved instantly. He'd been embarrassed. Because of her. He'd also been truly concerned she'd been kidnapped, and he had put his own pride on the line in order to do what had to be done to save her. She hadn't taken the protection order seriously, or that this man had a job and a responsibility: her.

From behind him, she put a hand on his shoulder,

trying to make a connection. He stiffened under her touch, and she took her hand away.

"I'm sorry," she said sincerely this time. "I panicked. I was trying to make things easier for myself, and I not only failed at that, but I put you, and Marco, for that matter, in a terrible, awkward position," she said, feeling more miserable by the minute. "I didn't mean to put you in that situation with your job or to make you worry. I never thought you would think I was kidnapped, but now I see how that would be the logical conclusion. I just wanted to…escape."

Chance turned, facing her. "From me?"

Now it was Ana's turn to look up at the treetops in frustration. For whatever reason, she couldn't look at him.

"You, at least as my bodyguard. I'm watched all the time, Chance. All day long, my life belongs to everyone, and there is no privacy. I accept that. It's the trade-off for my success. But this was supposed to be *my* time," she said, knowing still how selfish it all was. "And I wasn't ready for anyone to know about Marco."

"Me, you mean."

She nodded. "I wanted to escape it all. The show, the stalking, everything. All of it. Even this mess with Marco," she said, shaking her head. "But I didn't mean for you to be stuck in the middle of it, either. I should have dealt with him a long time ago, as well, but I kept putting it off, saying I was too busy."

Chance's expression became curious. "What mess?"

Ana shook her head, but his hands landed on her shoulders. It felt good, his touch. Maybe too good.

"Tell me, Ana. I need to know everything if I'm going to be able to do my job," he said, his gaze intent on hers.

Ana's mind blanked as her eyes fell to his mouth. They'd come so close on the plane...even closer in her dream. She swallowed her disappointment that he only seemed interested in terms of his job.

"Ana?"

When she looked back up, she caught her breath, saw the flicker of desire in his eyes, too. Maybe her disappointment was unfounded?

"Yes, okay, yes. I owe you that much, the truth," she said with a sigh, stepping back to break away from his touch so that she could think.

"Marco is my fiancé, though I never really accepted the engagement. When we were both young, our parents had decided we would marry," she explained, knowing how incredibly antiquated it all sounded.

"An arranged marriage?" Chance said in surprise. "They still do that?"

"Not generally, though you can still find the custom active in smaller villages. Marco's family is very old-fashioned, conservative, you might say. His parents held to the old ways out of respect for the grandparents, who insisted on an arranged marriage for the grandson. My father was his friend and wanted to help, so they made an agreement when we were only twelve that we would marry."

"Twelve?" Chance repeated, his eyes wide.

"Decades ago, we would have been married by the time I was fourteen. Marco and I grew up together—to be honest, he's more like a brother than anything else."

Chance snorted. "Yeah, right. I didn't get that impression."

"It's true. Marco has changed. He's not the boy I grew up with. I never really took any of this seriously. I figured they only made the arrangement to placate the elders, but then I left for college and my career, and no more was said about it. Marco has made his life, too, helping with his family business. He became an agricultural expert, and he travels the continent, helping local farmers improve their crops. But his grandfather is still living—he'll turn one hundred and two next month. Marco has come home and plans to make our engagement official before then, to honor his grandfather's wishes. I received a message to that effect a month ago, and I was as shocked as anyone."

"So you don't want to marry him?"

She shook her head vehemently. "No, of course not. And down deep, I don't believe he really wants to marry me. But now it's all so much more complicated."

"How so?"

"Well, our people have become quite modernized, but it would still be an embarrassment for me to just reject him—an insult—especially in his grandfather's eyes. And my family's reputation is at stake, as well. They have to live here after I go back to the States, and I also don't want to hurt an old friend. And then…well, there's you."

"Me? How do I fit into this?"

She looked at him pointedly. "I'm here, home, with another man. A man that I…desire," Ana said hesitantly.

Chance went still and his expression didn't change.

Ana had promised him the whole truth, so she delivered on that promise, whatever the consequences. "It makes everything more complicated, because while I know you are here only for a job, when we were on the plane, I felt something. A connection. I had thought that you felt it, too, and perhaps that there would be…more."

"More?" he echoed, his voice low and rougher in a way that rubbed over her skin.

She smiled a little. "I'm a modern woman, Chance, in spite of this strange situation with Marco. I've had lovers. I have a career. I don't intend on getting married or settling down, not anytime soon. But I'd hoped there could be more between us, at least while we were here."

They were closer now, standing only inches away in the deep shade of the trees, and everything was quiet around them except for the sounds of the birds and water flowing from the fountain at the edge of the garden.

She smiled again, with another self-effacing shake of her head. "So there you have it, the whole truth."

Chance seemed to consider what she'd told him and then stepped even closer.

"Thank you, Ana, for the truth. Here's mine," he said softly, lowering his head and taking her mouth in an unexpected kiss that wiped everything else from her mind.

His mouth was warm, hard and demanding, but he offered a kiss so perfect that it made her sigh, opening her lips so that they could explore each other further.

Chance's hands were on her back, pressing her close as he pressed her back against the broad trunk of a tree in the garden, trapping her against it as the kiss deepened and became even more...truthful. She wanted him, more than she had known, and now she knew that he wanted her, too.

Ana decided not to worry about how impossible that made everything as the kiss went on, losing herself in the moment.

CHANCE HAD BEEN CAUGHT off guard so many times in the past twelve hours that he wasn't sure which way was up, and feeling Ana's mouth on his, that sweet body pliant against him, made up for all of it. She might be playing him, manipulating him—it had occurred to him that he couldn't exactly trust her just then, given her actions—but he did trust her kiss. She didn't hold back, and neither did he.

"I knew you'd be delicious," he murmured against her mouth, returning for another kiss as his hand moved from her back to her waist and then upward to cover the swell of her breast. If she were merely trying to placate him, how far would she go?

But his doubts and suspicions were erased when he looked into her face and saw nothing but arousal and need. Her heart slammed against his palm as he touched her and swallowed her moan in a kiss as she arched against him.

He couldn't get enough of her, and anything else from the day evaporated in a mist of sheer need. There was nothing for Chance in that instant other than Ana's mouth, Ana's soft skin, Ana's sigh, Ana's hip pressing into his hardness.

Chance wanted only to push up her skirt and take her now, if not for what she'd just told him.

Ana was, technically, engaged.

She was also, very likely, still in danger.

He wanted to take her up against a tree in her family's backyard, anyway.

As if reinforcing his thoughts, she pulled back, murmured something and broke the kiss as the sound of a door echoed somewhere behind them.

"We...can't. Not here. Someone is home," she said, pushing him away more firmly as she ran a hand over her hair and smoothed her skirt.

Chance couldn't stop looking at her. "When?"

He shouldn't ask. Shouldn't even consider it, but he couldn't help himself.

"Shh," she shushed him with a sexy smile and passion-smudged eyes.

Then he saw why as she smiled widely and ran past him toward something—someone—else.

The woman in the courtyard who dropped her bags and opened her arms joyously could only be Ana's mother. Chance took a second to cool his jets as the two women embraced and said their hellos.

"And who is this?" Chance heard the older woman ask, glancing in his direction.

Both women turned to face him, and Chance saw where Ana got her beauty—her mother was striking, dressed in what he thought was likely a traditional, colorful sweep of fabric, with long, dark, shining hair and an older version of Ana's face. She was a bit taller than Ana and studied him with sharp, inquisitive eyes. The arm she draped around her daughter's shoulders was affectionate—and protective.

Ana led her mother across the courtyard to meet him, and he straightened up, smiling as he tried to clear his lust-fogged brain.

"Mama, this is Chance Berringer. He is a friend from the States. My plane was canceled, and Chance was good enough to use his personal plane to fly me home so that I would make it on time," she said, the lie falling from her lips so easily it bothered Chance a bit.

Then again, she couldn't tell her mother who he really was—he'd asked her not to do that, with anyone.

But worry that she'd been lying to him, too, still tightened his gut.

Was she lying about Marco, too? Playing some kind of game?

At the end of the day, Chance didn't know this woman at all. Still, he lived by his instincts. They had saved his life more than once, and he didn't really think Ana was lying to him.

She definitely hadn't faked the desire she'd felt in his arms.

*"Señora, encantado,"* Chance said, taking her mother's hand with a smile. "You have a lovely home, and Ana was just showing me around the gardens."

Senora Perez smiled warmly at him and covered his hand with her own, leaning in.

"Thank you for getting Ana home, Chance. It's good to know she has such good friends looking out for her. I hope you are staying a while?"

Ana glanced between them both. "Mama, I hoped Chance could stay through the holiday. He would not let me pay him for the flight, so I offered him a room, if that is all right?"

"Of course. I will ask Mariana to make up the guest room pronto," Señora Perez said and winked at Chance. "It will be fun to have a friend of Ana's around, and such a handsome one at that."

Chance laughed. "Thank you, and thank you for switching to English. Yours is flawless."

"Your Spanish is fine, but we speak several dialects here, and I enjoy English when I have an excuse to use it," the señora responded, drawing him to walk along with her on one side, and Ana on the other, back to the house. "How long have you and Ana been friends?"

Chance started to reply, but Ana cut in. He agreed it was probably better to let her set the cover story, and then he could just play along.

"A little while, Mama. Chance is a new hire by the studio, and we got to be friends."

"Flying Ana here is a big favor from a new friend," Señora Perez said with some degree of speculation in her tone, though she remained friendly enough. Still, her implication was clear.

Chance smiled. "I needed a vacation, and Ana needed to get home. It worked out," he said easily, hoping he was being completely convincing. "I didn't expect you to put me up, though. I could get a hotel room," he offered and hoped his gambit would work.

It did, as Ana's mother pooh-poohed his offer and insisted he stay with them.

That would make things easier on a number of counts.

"Gracias, Señora," Chance said sincerely.

"Call me Doncia, Chance. No need to be so formal," she responded, and Chance winked at Ana behind Doncia's back. He'd told her parents loved him.

Not that he'd met all that many parents of the women he'd dated, but some. And in high school and college, he'd perfected meeting the parents without raising anyone's expectations.

Though he supposed that Doncia's expectations and his were not at all the same. Better to keep that to himself.

"Mariana will show you your room while Ana and I catch up. Dinner is at seven. Everyone will be here, and they will love to meet you, as well," Doncia told him as she nodded to him and then turned away, still linked at the arm with Ana.

Chance was grateful for a break. The shadows of early evening were stretching across the house and yard, and he wanted to make a survey of the property before everyone got home. Following Mariana, one of Ana's younger cousins, to his room, he was impressed with the gorgeous view from a small veranda outside of the spacious bedroom. No doubt all of this was due to Ana's success.

She had kept only a living salary from her considerable TV income, investing the rest in the village, financing businesses and, clearly, buying her family a nice home. She was generous, a giving person who clearly cared about others.

Chance felt selfish by comparison, always preferring to follow his own whims, his own adventures. He cared about his family and friends—and his work, of course. But while Berringer Bodyguards supported several nonprofit organizations through their business and even took on pro bono work, he knew that he'd led a charmed life with only himself, for the most part, to worry about.

He preferred not to think about others who worried about *him,* like his parents or his brothers. They knew who he was, he thought a little uncomfortably. He even recalled the look in his mother's eyes once when he had barely escaped from a burning race car he had crashed while taking a few laps at a local track.

The memory of how rattled he'd been by Logan's accident and then the thought of losing Ana that afternoon came rushing back; but that was hardly the same. Logan was a friend, and Ana was his client.

He switched gears away from the reflective, and uncomfortable, train of thought and focused on the scene before him. The area all around the house was shaded and blocked by trees and plants, which could allow anyone to approach unseen, hidden from various directions. He'd noticed a few dogs out back, but they hadn't even seemed very concerned with his arrival.

Quietly leaving his room, he slipped along the cool, exposed breezeway that opened up the middle of the second floor and headed down a spiral staircase to the grounds below.

It was beautiful, he had to admit, as he assessed access points to the house. He had no idea which bedroom was Ana's—which he would need to know, of course— for purely professional reasons.

As enticing as it might be to think about slipping into her room at night, even Chance wouldn't try to be with her under her mother's roof—and while she was technically engaged—even though clearly the engagement was a sham. Still, there was something about Marco that bothered him, and he hoped Ana called off the engagement soon.

Chance spent another half hour or so investigating every part of the property that he could and making a mental note of escape routes, possible dangers and any other number of routine checks.

Looking up, he paused, seeing Ana on a balcony of her own—that had to be her room. She simply stood there and gazed out over the gardens. What was she thinking?

He was hidden by the trees, so he took a minute to watch her. His heart beat noticeably faster, his chest tightening, body hardening.

What was it about this woman that tied him in knots and all he had to do was look at her?

Blowing out a breath, he turned to head back in and found himself face-to-face with Marco, who stood silently behind him.

It had been a long, long time since anyone had gotten the drop on Chance, and he wasn't happy about it. Yet, he tried to relax, even offering a smile.

"Marco. Nice to see you again. I thought you had

gone…somewhere," Chance said congenially, shoving his hands, previously tensed to fight, into his pockets.

"I came back. What are you doing out here, watching Ana?"

"I wasn't. I was taking a walk, checking the place out."

"Why?"

Chance shrugged. "Why not? I wanted to get acquainted with where I'm staying for the next few weeks."

Marco's face became dark. "Here? You are staying here with Ana?"

"I am. Well, not with her, but with her family. Her mother invited me," Chance explained. "And I couldn't say no."

Marco stepped toward him. "I see the look in your eyes, how much you want her. But Ana is mine."

Chance pursed his lips, stood his ground. "I think Ana is…Ana's."

Chance was sorely tempted to tell the guy to cancel his wedding plans, but that wasn't his place; it was Ana's. So without another word, he stepped around Marco and returned to the house.

"There are a lot of dangers here, Mr. Berringer. Things Americans don't understand," Marco said after him.

Chance paused. "Are you threatening me, Marco? Because I'd think twice about doing that."

"I don't know why you are here, but I don't believe you are Ana's friend. You want…something else."

Chance decided not to confirm or deny the statement and simply mock saluted the other man before striding away. But his mind replayed the incident, Marco's silent approach, his body language and his words, all the way back to his room. This wasn't good.

Delightful aromas filled the house, but he was pre-occupied with thoughts of Marco. Chance had done a thorough assessment of the danger points around the house, but what about the ones inside? The people closest to Ana?

Something told him, he thought, as he lay back on the soft bed to relax and think before dinner, that when it came to Ana, there was a lot to consider.

# 6

ANA WAS EXACTLY WHERE SHE wanted to be, but she wasn't enjoying herself at all. Tension was tight all down her spine, her head pounding as she smiled and visited with her family. She was all too aware of Marco's large presence nearby almost every second. He had glued himself to her side and wasted no excuse to touch her, although he did so politely. Marco would not be otherwise in front of her family.

Ana only wanted one man's touch and met Chance's eyes across the courtyard, where he sat having a bite to eat and talking with her young cousin Juan. Juan was only seventeen but had plans to go to school in the States. He was very excited to talk to Chance about East Coast schools. To his credit, Chance seemed equally interested and engaged as he spoke to the young man, and Ana appreciated that.

But as Marco's hand fell to the small of her back, she reached around, closing her own around it, and removed it.

"Marco, we have to talk. Alone," she said, knowing that she had to do this now. She couldn't let it go any further.

His eyes were intent on her, almost making her look away. "Yes," he said smoothly. "It would be nice to be alone."

*Oh, no,* Ana thought miserably. *It won't be nice at all.*

He was a good man. He had often looked in on her mother and helped with family things while she was gone. And he'd taken on that role without being asked. Ana owed him a certain amount of affection and respect for that alone. She needed to show him she had respect for him by making herself clear now.

However, when a flurry of excitement rose on the other side of the yard, distracting her, a cry of joy went up and Ana spotted her sister, Lucia, whom she hadn't seen in months.

"I didn't know you were coming," Ana said, squeezing her sister tight.

Lucia looked lovely, though exhausted.

"You've lost weight," Ana said, studying her sister's face.

Lucia laughed. "You sound like Mama now."

"Are you okay?"

"I'm fine. Work is hard, long days, and we do not have *caramel de leche* every day, you know, like some people," her sister teased.

"Huh. Are you saying I'm fat?" Ana responded, teasing her sister.

"I'm saying you're gorgeous and I want you to make me your famous *caramel de leche,*" Lucia said, laughing.

"I'm so glad to see you," Ana said, kissing her sister and meeting Marco's eyes over her sister's shoulder. He took them in, warm emotion in his gaze.

Ana hated to hurt him.

"Come in and sit. We have a lot to catch up on," Ana said, drawing her sister to the table. The earlier awkwardness with Marco dissolved in the happiness and bustle of the evening. Chance was being kept busy by two more of her younger cousins. He fit right in, she realized and watched for just a second longer.

"So who is he?" Lucia whispered, leaning in as she followed the trajectory of Ana's gaze.

"A friend," Ana said lamely.

Lucia snorted. "We should all have such handsome friends."

"Shh. Marco will hear."

Lucia became serious. "So you are going through with it? Marrying him?"

"No, of course not. I was about to talk to him before you arrived. I will tell him tonight, before he goes."

"That is good. I don't know why Papa ever promised you and made that arrangement, but Marco takes it very seriously."

"I know. I should have addressed this sooner, but I suppose I thought he would just move on."

"Men like Marco...everything for them is family, duty, honor. They do not move on so easily," Lucia said with a sigh.

Ana knew she was right and chastised herself for having left things hanging like this. It showed how much she had become part of her new life, letting the threads that held her here weaken. That was something she was going to change.

"No more about that. Please, tell me everything about you, where you have been, what you are doing."

Lucia brightened and told Ana of her positive experiences in her work. Ana was glad to hear her sister was now home for the entire vacation. She had missed her so much.

"I worry about you being safe out there," Ana said, laying her hand over her sister's.

"It can be dangerous. More so these days, it seems. We interfere, and a lot of people have not been happy with that. But the people suffer and so need our help," Lucia said.

"You are so brave." Ana felt her throat tighten at her sister's sacrifice for so many people.

"Not so much. I had to leave, and I may not be able to go back. It was getting too dangerous. Not just for myself but for those we were helping. One cartel in particular has targeted us, and they would not hesitate to take it out on the people," Lucia confessed, looking very sad.

"They are a scourge," Ana said hotly, hating the thought of her sister being afraid. "But there are plenty of places for you to help, I'm sure. I am thinking about not going back, as well. At least, not to the show."

Lucia's eyes reflected her shock, but their conversation was cut short when Ana felt a hand on her shoulder. Looking up, she saw Marco.

"May I steal Ana away to say good-night? I have an early morning tomorrow," he said, leaning down to hug Lucia, as well.

"Yes, of course," Lucia said, squeezing Ana's hand in silent support.

Ana walked with Marco to a quiet alcove by the front of the house, where, ensconced in shadow, she tried to find the right words.

He took her silence for something other, and before she could stop him, he kissed her, shocking her completely. Ana pushed him away, which surprised him, too.

"Marco, I'm sorry. I didn't mean to react that way. It's just been—"

"A long time, I know, Ana. But we can make up for lost time now. I thought we would make our plans final on the New Year, so that our families can all celebrate with us. I'm afraid I will have to leave on business again shortly after that, but you will be back to the States, too. We will have to work out the details," he added, clearly having thought about this more than she had.

Ana took a deep breath, steeling her spine.

"I'm so sorry, Marco," she repeated. "But I'm not going to marry you. I should have told you years ago, but I never imagined you held to the promise our fathers made when we were children. Not until I heard from you," she said in a rush, while she had the nerve. "I consider you a friend. A dear friend, but...I am not in love with you. And my life, much of it, is in the States. And if nothing else, your work and your life are here. Even if I wanted to go through with it, it would never work."

Silence hung heavily between them, and Marco's voice was low as he stepped closer. Not the move she'd anticipated, and she felt herself backed against the cool adobe wall.

"Is it this man? Chance? He is your lover?"

Ana blinked at the anger in his tone. Somehow, she had expected his disappointment at most, but not his anger.

"No, but if it was, it's none of your business. I've lived my life on my own for over a decade, Marco, and it's how I intend to keep living it. You and I, we have hardly spoken in that time, so why now? Why send that message now? You never gave me any indication you wanted to see this childhood promise through."

Ana could hear his breathing, see his eyes flash as

he looked down at her. Then he turned away, his posture stiff. He was a proud man, she knew. And Lucia was right—he was old-fashioned. She should have seen it coming.

"I'm afraid it's not that easy," Marco said.

"What do you mean?"

"I need to marry to inherit my family's business. My grandfather will not will it to me if we do not honor our promise."

Ana's eyes widened. "You want to marry me so that you can get the family store?"

"You make it sound so cheap. It is not. I respect you, and I would be a good husband. It would embarrass my grandfather, my family greatly, for us not to marry. They would not forgive me. I would look like a failure in their eyes. You must honor this promise, Ana."

Ana shook her head, unsure what to think. "I don't know what to say. *I* never made a promise, Marco. My father did, and he shouldn't have. But I'm not marrying you, and you have to accept that. I'm sorry, but your family will have to work this out among themselves."

He spun, advancing on her. "You disclaim your heritage, your family's duty, so easily? You cast aside any responsibility you have to them like this? To me? For what? For the American? For your life there, you sacrifice your life here?"

Ana's own temper rose, and she pushed him back again, and she didn't apologize for it this time.

"Watch yourself, Marco. We're friends, and I want us to stay that way, but I won't be treated like anyone's property."

He pulled her close to him, and Ana's breath escaped in a gasp of pain.

"Marco, stop it," she said and, a second later, felt his grip loosen as he was pulled backward, away from her.

Ana thought at first that he'd fallen, tripped, but then she saw Chance hauling him back and facing off with Marco, his expression fierce.

"Chance, no," Ana gasped as the two men grappled and punches were thrown, both of them falling to the hard surface of the patio as others came rushing to see what was happening. Ana heard her mother's and Lucia's shocked exclamations.

Two of her cousins moved forward to try to break up the brawling men, but her mother put a hand out, stopping them. It was the right thing to do—her younger cousins were no match for these two large, angry men.

"I don't know how you do things down here, but *no* means *no*, Marco," Chance said, once he had Marco in a tight throat hold.

Marco struggled for a second and then flipped Chance over, making him land hard on his back. Ana stepped forward and then caught her mother's eye, too.

"You know nothing of this," Marco ground out. "You have no say."

"Maybe not," Chance agreed. "But if you think I was going to stand by and let you try to push her around, think again."

"And what were you doing, exactly, watching from the shadows? What business of this is yours?" Marco accused.

The two men growled and raised their fists again, and this time, Ana did step forward.

*"Alto!"* she commanded and ran between the two men before they exchanged blows. "Stop this immediately!"

To her shock, they did, heaving breaths like angry bulls on each side of her, but stopping all the same.

"Marco, I'm so sorry, but I do not want to marry you," she said, hating to embarrass him publicly, but he had certainly contributed to that. "And, Chance, I will not have this kind of behavior from anyone in my family's home."

Ana's tone was clear and she made eye contact with both men to let them know she meant business.

"I'm sorry, Ana. You're right, of course," Chance said, setting off flickers of heat in her bloodstream.

"Yes, he is so noble. Sleeping with a woman promised to another."

"We are *not* sleeping together," Ana said emphatically, feeling her cheeks burn as she defended herself in front of God and everyone. "That comment was uncalled for, as is your behavior, Marco."

Instead of apologizing, Marco sent them both a dark look and stormed off.

Ana looked at Chance, noting the bruise on his cheek and the tear in his shirt. Other than that, he seemed no worse for wear. Looking past him, she made eye contact with her mother.

"I am so sorry, Mama. I never thought this would happen," she said, walking forward to take her mother's hands.

"It is very upsetting, *hermosa,* but we can talk about it in the morning. For now, it is late, and there has been enough excitement," Doncia said, though her attention was on Chance, rather than Ana.

Ana couldn't read her mother's expression, if it was disapproval or appreciation, or something else, but she nodded her agreement. In her heart, Ana had a feel-

ing this was not going to be the relaxing trip home
that she thought it would be.

CHANCE GRIMACED AS HE STEPPED out of the shower
and took in the deepening purple of the bruise on his
cheek. Marco had a fist like Ironman, and that punch
had nearly knocked him out. But the vision of the guy
pushing Ana up against the wall had more than moti-
vated Chance to get up and respond, hit for hit.

In retrospect, maybe not the best move. He'd lost his
head for a minute and had forgotten his role as bodyguard, driven by pure male instinct to defend Ana in a
much more personal way.

Marco had known. And Chance couldn't blame the
guy for being upset—it sucked to be dumped, but especially with so much riding on the marriage. It was
archaic but unfortunate that Marco stood to lose more
than his bride, but that wasn't Ana's responsibility.

Wrapping a towel around his waist, he went into
the bedroom and lay down, letting a cool breeze from
the screened windows drift over his still-damp skin.
When he'd left Ana, she was with her mother and sister, picking up after the party. She was safe, and he
needed to think.

There was still something about Marco that kept itch-
ing at Chance. He was strong as a bull, but he knew how
to fight, and not just instinctively—he'd been trained.

Chance wondered if a new element had been added
into the mix.

The male part of his brain was focused on the reality that Ana was now completely free of any obligation to Marco. His mind traveled back to the kiss in the
courtyard and how soft she was, but how hot, as well.

She said she wanted more with him. It wasn't advisable, but there were worse ways to stay close to his principal.

Drifting off, Chance finally gave in to the urge to sleep, something he hadn't done for days. Sensual images of Ana infiltrated his dreams. Her hands, her mouth...until a distant sound had him awake, sitting upright, staring at the door.

The knob was turning, slowly, silently, as if not to be heard. It was well after midnight, the house silent, Ana's family sleeping. Whoever this was, they weren't invited.

Chance stood, hugging the wall by the door, hardly breathing as he waited.

The door opened slightly, and someone stepped in.

He moved quickly from behind, knowing from the moment his hands touched her, and his nose caught the scent of her hair, who it was in his grasp.

"Ana?" he whispered, letting go and shutting the door quietly.

She stood in the soft light of his room, looking at him with those big brown eyes, her hair slightly messy, as if she had just left her own bed. She wore a thin, cream-colored shift that—God help him—showed the lovely silhouette of her naked form underneath the fabric.

"What are you doing here? I could have hurt you," he said, not taking one step closer.

For the first time since he'd met her, Ana Perez looked uncertain.

"I couldn't sleep. I'm sorry. I...I shouldn't have come. I don't know what I was thinking," she said, nervous. "I'm sorry," she repeated. "Good night."

Chance stopped her with a hand on her shoulder before she could turn the knob.

"Ana, what *were* you thinking?"

He was so close, standing right next to her, that her

scent seemed to surround him, hypnotizing him. He drew her against him, his hands on her shoulders, his mouth by her ear.

"Were you thinking about me?" he whispered.

She nodded, swallowing hard. "I wanted to make sure you were okay," she said softly, shifting in his arms. She raised a hand to his face, touching his bruise gingerly. "And to thank you."

"For what?"

"For helping," she said with a slight smile.

"I should have stopped the fight," he said, rubbing his chin lightly along her hairline, making her close her eyes and tip her head back for more. "I'm sorry I let it go that far."

"Thank you," she said, offering her lips up for a kiss that blotted out anything else. Pulling her up against him, his arms closed around her, the two of them pressed together completely.

"You were thinking about this?" he asked roughly before his tongue took to investigating her bottom lip.

"Yes."

It was what he wanted to hear.

"Me, too. I couldn't get this afternoon out of my head," he admitted, as hungry as she was. Lifting her thigh, she slid her leg against his, opening so that her body brought his erection even closer to her core. Chance groaned, pressing in.

"Ana," he said on a choked breath, sliding his hands into her hair and holding her still as he dived back in for a deeper kiss, his tongue exploring, tangling with hers as she did the same to him.

She tasted so good, he thought vaguely, as she let him hold her and move her any way he pleased. It was wonderful as his hands cupped her bottom, grinding her against him, and she shuddered with need as he brought her very close to coming but then loosened his hold.

She moaned a little in protest, and he pulled her up so that she was no longer standing but had to wrap her arms and legs around him and hold on. His towel had hit the floor, and he caught his breath on a choked curse, feeling her against him.

Perfect, as he knew she would be.

Her nightgown had pushed up with the movement, so she was bare against him except for the slick, thin material of the thong she wore. Chance reached back, twisting the material in his hands and tearing it from her body with one firm pull, making her gasp in pleasure.

He didn't want anything between them and let go with one hand to try to lift the thin shift from her body, but it was caught, and Ana helped, so that she was as naked as he was.

Ana kissed him this time, her nipples rubbing against the light bit of hair on his chest. She swayed back and forth to intensify the contact as she kissed him as deeply as he had kissed her.

"I can barely keep it together. I might end up disappointing you," he said with a faint chuckle, leading her to the bed.

"Not possible." She smiled, squeezing his hand.

He set her down on the edge of the massive bed and grabbed his duffel, taking out several small, round foil packets.

"I hadn't even thought of that," she admitted. "But I am…safe. Protected."

"Never hurts to be sure," he said.

Ana stopped him just short of sitting on the bed with her and turned him to her.

"Let me see you," she said, her eyes on him.

Chance held still, held his breath, wondering what was next. Hoping.

Her hand ran up the inside of his strong thigh to cup him and then stroke along the soft skin beneath. He trembled and groaned, a hand landing on her shoulder to steady himself.

"Ana," he said on an unsteady breath as her fingers explored, traveling over his length.

She leaned forward to press a kiss to his flat, taught belly, and he said her name again, reverently. Ana smiled, still holding him in her hand, and dipped her lips down to kiss him intimately, letting her tongue sweep over the tip of his cock.

Sensation so sharp he almost felt split in two drove through him, and he cursed on a sharp exhale, hearing her soft, satisfied chuckle. Ana tasted him more thoroughly, and before she was done, he was shaking, his knees starting to give out as he got closer to coming.

"Ana, stop, or this is going to be over before it starts," he said, panting and reaching for a foil packet.

She took it from him and covered him herself, her touch making him close his eyes, hold his breath.

She knew what he wanted, and pushed back on the bed so that he could get between her thighs and pull her forward to the edge. She was so ready, and Chance swallowed hard, not taking his eyes from hers as he poised his cock at the swell of her sex, touching, sliding, teasing.

Ana arched off the bed, her hands on her breasts like his fantasy come to life. He eased inside of her, just a bit, and she cried out, begging him for more.

"Ana, you undo me" was all he said before he dipped down to replace her fingers, taking her nipple in his mouth, drawing on her hard as he pressed the rest of himself into her. He looked up then, breathing hard as he stayed planted deep inside.

She caught his eye, her own breath labored now. "Someone might hear. Have to be quiet," he said with a smile, nodding to the open windows.

She smiled back, nodding in agreement.

He returned to her breast, which had her writhing on the bed, biting her lip as he started to move inside her. He suckled her to the same rhythm of his thrusts, loving how she twined her fingers through his hair.

The tempo of his thrusts quickened, and she moaned and sighed, telling him that she was enjoying the ride. Every muscle in his body went rigid as she closed around him, pulsing tight and drawing his release even closer. He slowed down, wanted to last.

Framing his face in her hands, she looked into his eyes. "Make me come, Chance… Let go… Just take me like you want to," she said.

It was as if something snapped inside of him, and he stood, tugging her forward, his hands holding her delectable ass as she wrapped her legs around his lower back. He pressed into her faster, wilder, like a hot wire broken free.

"Ana," he growled under his breath, his body straining when she leaned into him, keening with pleasure as her tight muscles pulsed around his cock. As she climaxed, she clung to him as he set off yet another hot wave of release through her body.

Chance was aware of nothing but the pleasure he felt being inside her, unaware of anything but the searing satisfaction of his own climax as it rushed along every inch of his body. As the most intense moments passed, he let her go, fell forward over her, braced on his arms.

"Ana, if I died right now, that would be okay," he

said, but he was grinning when he tilted his forehead against hers.

Chance had made love to a lot of women, but he was damned sure not one of them had completely wrecked him as Ana had. Nothing had ever been like this.

"No, it really wouldn't be," she joked as she kissed him. "I'm not nearly done with you yet," she added with a smile.

Music to his ears.

# 7

THUNDER RUMBLED SOMEWHERE in the distance, and rain started to patter softly outside as Ana thought about how much things could change in a day.

She hadn't been sure about coming to Chance's room, offering herself to him, but as she'd tossed and turned in bed, he was all she could think of. Wanting him, and wanting something that would obliterate every other thought, worry and concern in her head.

He had certainly done that.

She watched him walk to the bathroom, returning a few seconds later to lay back down beside her.

"What are you thinking about now?" he asked.

She raised her eyebrows and answered truthfully. "About doing it again."

He laughed. "You might have to give me a little recovery time. You wrung me dry."

"I can wait," she said, rolling over to cover him, folding her arms on her chest and resting her chin there, gazing out at the rain.

He was warm, big and solid. Ana cuddled into him,

resting the sensitive apex of her thighs against his hard abdomen. She sighed in satisfaction.

"Storm moving in," he commented absently.

"A small one. Our rainy season isn't until the summer months, and then, of course, there is hurricane season," she said with a shudder.

"You've been caught in one?"

"A few times. No way to miss it down here. I bought this house for my family—reinforced brick—because everything we had was lost in 2005, with Wilma," she said, remembering the carnage.

"You take good care of them," he said, arms behind his head as he looked out the window with her. She liked the intimacy that the rain pattering on the window created between them, as if there was no one else in the world.

"I wanted them to come back to the States with me, but this is home. My father died that year, as well," she said, swallowing hard as she remembered that sadness.

"In the hurricane?"

She shook her head. "Heart attack, just before. The hurricane just added insult to injury, but that year…it was hard, to say the least."

"You had just agreed to a contract for your cable show in 2005, right?"

"*Sí.* It meant I had to be away from home much more than I should have been. I wish I had seen Papa more. I wish—"

She stopped, taking a deep breath and shaking her head. "This is not what we should be talking about," she said, leaning down to take a flat nipple between her teeth, sucking lightly and liking the sound he made in response.

"You do a lot for your family, for your village," he

said as his hands traveled over her shoulders, her back. "What do you do for Ana?"

She smiled, turning in his arms. "Those things are for me, too. They make me happy. I have a wonderful life," she said, rising, her hands on his chest.

Ana wanted him again and felt his answer against the inside of her thigh. Still, it was nice to talk, too. To be just two people, making love, getting to know each other, and nothing more.

"You've built up half of this village or more. Financed most of the small businesses," he said, kissing her temple.

"How do you know— Oh, the file," she said, remembering. "What else would I do with the money? Fast cars and faster men?" she joked.

"Something like that," he offered with a grin.

"I take care of my family, and I take care of myself," she said, leveling him a look, rocking against him gently.

Ana was quickly losing interest in the conversation and eyed the remaining packets on the bed.

"In a little while. Soon," Chance promised, his eyes on her, knowing what she wanted.

Maybe knowing what she wanted more than she did, as he grabbed her hips and urged her forward, positioning her over his mouth.

Ana quivered with excitement, anticipating his touch. He didn't make her wait, and she didn't worry about making noise as the storm rose.

"Oh, Chance, yes, please," she begged as he took her clit in between his lips, sucking as his fingers explored her slick flesh.

Ana closed her eyes, letting the storm and the mounting pleasure consume her. Chance rolled his tongue around her tender flesh, sucking and lapping at her as his fingers teased her with tender, sensitive touches. She tensed.

"No?" he whispered against the inside of her thigh, waiting.

"Yes," she whispered.

Returning his mouth to her, his fingers explored and tested, gently finding his way inside her. Ana was lost in the host of new sensations taking over her body. And when he pushed deeper, sucked a little harder, she lost it completely. Thrashing over him, she came harder than she would have imagined was possible, losing track of everything but the pleasure he sent crashing through her. She wasn't sure how long it lasted, but she didn't want it to end.

As her pleasure receded, she sought more, sliding down his body to cover him again. He was so hard, so *big*. Planting her hands on his chest, she lowered herself over him, taking him fully inside as she watched his face contort. His lips expelled her name on a harsh breath as he jacked his hips up under her.

"Come with me, Chance," she said, as she danced seductively over him, her head back, her breasts thrust toward him.

An explosion of wind and booming sound from outdoors crashed around them as their harsh cries filled the room, mingling with the noise around them. Ana's wild ride settled to a slow, easy rocking as their passion cooled, and Chance reached down, sliding a finger in between her thighs to caress her. He watched her closely as her body shuddered over his with one more impossibly sweet climax.

He held her close, pulling a blanket over them as the air from the storm chilled their heated bodies. She was half-asleep as he pulled her in, tucking her into his body. Ana released a long breath and slept the best sleep of her life.

ANA AWOKE WITH A SMILE as she realized that she was alone in Chance's bed. The storm had passed and sunlight glittered off the leaves and plants that surrounded the veranda.

Checking the clock, her eyes widened. She'd slept very late. Well, late for her. Chance should have awakened her, but then again, if he had, they would likely still be in bed, anyway, she thought, grinning.

Chance had been amazing. He'd excited her like no other lover she'd had.

What a night it had been. Her body felt tender from use but totally relaxed as only a passionate night of sex with a wonderful man could make happen. She wanted more. Much more, but that was for later.

Now she had to focus on her family, the holiday and all of the other reasons she was here. Slipping from under the blankets, her feet landed on the cool tile floor as she picked up her nightgown, gave it a shake before she put it back on.

Voices rang from below, someone down in the garden. Hopefully, she could get over to her room unnoticed. Surely, everyone was awake by now.

No such luck.

She practically smashed into her sister coming around the corner to the hallway where Lucia's room was next to hers.

"Lucia, good morning," Ana said, laughing and hoping her sister wouldn't think anything of her running around the hall in her flimsy nightgown.

Interestingly, Lucia also looked disheveled, though

she was fully dressed. Ana studied her face for a moment—something about her seemed different. Her face flushed, her eyes a little glassy. Was Lucia ill?

"Are you okay?"

"I'm fine, why?" Lucia's response was quick and curt, and Ana frowned.

"I'm sorry. I didn't sleep well, and I went for a run. You know how it always leaves me agitated. What are you doing?" her sister asked more reasonably, with an inquiring eyebrow as she took in Ana's dress.

Ana closed her arms over her middle, not that that would hide anything.

"I needed to get some aspirin from the main bath," she said, the lie falling from her lips more easily than she liked, but no way was she letting anyone know what she had been doing last night.

Not even Lucia.

"I see," Lucia said softly and nodded agreeably before moving past Ana. "Are you well?"

"Just a little headache."

"Well, I am going downstairs for some breakfast. You will be down soon?"

Ana smiled, glad that her sister was letting her off the hook, even if Lucia didn't seem to completely buy her story.

"In just a few minutes."

Lucia smiled and left, and Ana ducked into her room unseen by anyone else.

It felt so illicit—sneaking into a man's bedroom in her family home. It was…inappropriate, even at her age, but she didn't regret a second of her time with Chance.

As she quickly showered and dressed, she exited her room again, heading downstairs. The familiar, succulent scent of her mother's cooking led her to the kitchen, where Doncia was working at the counter.

Ana smiled. Her mother always cooked for her when she was home. It was an overwhelming treat, as much as Ana loved to cook, to have someone present *her* with a meal. Her mother's cooking was second to none, not even her own.

"Mama, this smells wonderful," she said, crossing the kitchen to hug her mother.

"You slept in," her mother said, kissing her forehead and studying her face, maybe too closely.

Ana averted her eyes. "I was tired. The show has been nonstop for weeks," she said, cleaning a spot on the counter where her mother had been chopping vegetables.

"Hmm. It was upsetting with Marco last night," Doncia said.

"Yes." Ana sighed. "But necessary."

Her mother sighed, too. "If you do not love him, then that is best."

Ana paused, somewhat surprised by her mother's easy agreement.

"You are not upset with me?"

It was her mother's turn to look surprised.

"Why would I be upset with you, Ana? You must do what your heart tells you, whether it is with your life work or to whom you give your heart," she said.

"Thank you, Mama," Ana said with no small amount of relief.

It lasted only a second.

"And Chance, he was also all right after last night's… conflict?"

Ana paused. She had spent time in the kitchen with

her family, cleaning up after the party, and Chance had gone to his room to tend to his wounds.

Her mother was crafty, Ana thought appreciatively.

"I assume he was fine," Ana said lightly, carrying a plate of fruit to the table.

"Ana."

Ana knew that tone.

"Mama, really," she started, but Doncia interrupted her.

"I saw how he looks at you—like you are everything. The only thing he sees. And how he fought for you last night," Doncia said with a fond smile. "Your father looked at me like that. Fought for me once, too," she added.

"Papa? Fight?" Ana said, distracted by that bit of information. Her father was a gardener, a peace-loving man. She couldn't imagine him ever raising a fist.

"There was another man. He wanted me, though I was in love with your papa. This other man, Arturo, would not take no. He did, after your father made it very clear to keep his distance," Doncia said happily. "Much like your...friend."

Ana swallowed hard. How to tell her mother that Chance was only so focused on her because she was his client? That he watched her so intently, and protected her, because that was his job?

He had told her not to tell anyone, and Ana felt trapped. Her mother had the entirely wrong idea.

"I saw him kiss you in the courtyard yesterday," her mother added, sealing the statement with a damning look. Ana's goose was cooked. "He's a good man. *Es puro de espíritu.* I could see that right away about him."

"Okay, Mama. Yes, we are…attracted to each other, but it's nothing serious. Not like you and Papa."

As the words left her lips, she looked up to notice Chance in the doorway to the kitchen.

"Chance. *Buenos días,*" she said, and her mother turned to wish him the same, with a welcoming smile.

"Come, sit. I've kept some breakfast warm. You and Ana were both very tired after everything that happened last night," Doncia said, innocently as could be, but Ana sent her mother a warning look.

"Is there anything I can do to help?" Chance offered, smiling at Ana in a way that she felt down to her toes. Her mother's back was to them. The look he sent her told her that he was thinking about everything that had happened between them the night before.

Worse, her mother would know everything in an instant, and then she would hear wedding bells ringing again, when all Chance was…what? Convenient? Hot? Willing?

All of those, Ana thought guiltily. So she had met him in the night and scratched an itch? So what? Men did it all the time, she thought to herself as she finished setting the table as Chance chatted with her mother in easy Spanish.

"I always make huevos rancheros for Ana when she comes home. She has to cook all of the time with her job, so I like her to enjoy being cooked for when she visits. Although most of her famous recipes are mine and her *abuela's,* my mother Paula's," Doncia told Chance, while showing him how to mince the jalapeños easily and safely.

"They have inspired all of my own," Ana added affectionately. "A new book of them, even."

Chance turned to her. "You're having another book published?"

Ana smiled, glad to change topics. "It's titled *Recipes from Home,* and it's been a labor of love. I work on it when I have time away from the show, and I just delivered it to the publisher at Christmas. I dedicated it to you, Mama, and Mama Paula," she said, smiled at the shocked look on her mother's face.

"Oh, Ana! That's wonderful," her mother said warmly.

Ana knew what her mother really wanted was grandchildren, and worried that neither of her daughters would produce that boon within her lifetime. Ana couldn't make any promises, but she was glad her mother was excited—hopefully, over her professional accomplishments.

"I hoped that you would write the forward to it, Mama, while I am here. Maybe you could write about how you taught all of us to cook when we were children," Ana suggested.

Her mother's eyes filled and she started rattling off so much so fast in Spanish that Chance looked totally bemused. Ana laughed, enveloping her mother in a hug.

"Mama, you will have plenty to say. It will be *our* book—mine, yours and Mama Paula's, because I could never have done any of this without you," Ana said, feeling her own eyes burn.

Ana was glad to have her mother thinking about something other than her and Chance, and she smiled as she caught his attention.

He smiled and winked in her direction, making her heart melt. Had he heard her say they had nothing serious? She could only assume he was okay with that.

They'd known each other for only forty-eight hours, and not even that. How could they have anything else?

Though in some ways, they knew each other very well. He knew just how to touch her to send her pulse skyrocketing and how to kiss her so exquisitely like no man ever had. He knew she wasn't completely happy with her current job and that she wanted to go back to simpler things. He knew she didn't like being watched or controlled, and he knew how to make her heart beat faster with only a look.

The moment was broken when the kitchen suddenly was full of voices as her cousins and then...Marco walked in.

CHANCE STEPPED AWAY FROM the counter, watching Marco carefully. The big man had a bruised eye, almost closed, and Chance hardly remembered getting the punch in.

Marco met his gaze and stiffened, his back straight, clearly tense.

"Doncia, Ana," he said. "Mr. Berringer."

Chance nodded in his direction but made it clear that he was ready for another go around if it was needed.

"I'm glad to catch you all here, in one place. I came to apologize for my behavior in your home," he said to Doncia, with a slight bow, a downward look and then to Ana, "and to you and your guest. How I behaved was unacceptable, under any circumstances, even considering my surprise at Ana's rejection," he said, his cheeks reddening with embarrassment.

Chance actually felt bad for the guy.

Ana rose from her seat at the table and took both of Marco's hands in hers. "Marco, I didn't reject you. You are a wonderful man, but we were never meant to be together. We never have been together. So there can be no rejection, right? You are always welcome here, and a part of our family, no matter what."

Marco's face softened a bit as he looked down at Ana.

"*Gracias,* Ana. That is very gracious of you."

"She says what we all feel, Marco. Come have some breakfast," Doncia said, and Chance smiled at the easy forgiveness, the genuine warmth. These were good people. All of them, even Marco.

As things relaxed, he stepped forward, putting his hand out.

"For what it's worth, you have some pretty slick moves in a fight," Chance said, wincing as he touched his sore cheek with his other hand and smiling as Marco took his hand in a firm shake.

"You, as well. I haven't let anyone blacken my eye since I was seven years old," Marco said with grudging respect.

"You learned to fight like that just, you know, around?" Chance asked, but he was also fishing.

"Somewhat. I was also in the Mexican police force for years, and the military. I retired to help my family with the business and to focus on my life here as my parents got older," he said.

"And to help after Papa died," Ana added, gratitude evident in her tone.

"Happily. José was a close friend of my father's, like a brother. We are all family," he affirmed.

Doncia announced that the food was done, and what appeared to be the second breakfast of the morning was served. Chance was grateful—he was starving.

He'd woken up early, tempted to wake Ana, as well, but he also wanted to take advantage of the early hour to go check out the town, and did so under the guise of taking an early-morning run. Doncia had been up cooking then, too, for the members of the family who were heading out to work early.

Right now, the tension with Marco settled, Chance was thankful for the chaos around him; it kept him from thinking too much about what he'd heard Ana say as he arrived in the kitchen, and how she had avoided his gaze. She was clearly uncomfortable. He supposed it was only natural, given that she was among her family.

Even so, he couldn't look at her without remembering how she tasted, how soft she was and how she had exploded around him. She was right. They had a moment, a night—an experience that hopefully would be repeated—but it wasn't more than that.

Not serious at all.

What he hadn't told her, and wasn't sure how to understand for himself, was the red-hot rage he'd felt when Marco had advanced on her when she told him she wasn't going to marry him. If Marco had touched her at all—seeing him kiss her had been bad enough—Chance wasn't sure he wouldn't have done more than blacken the man's eye.

Chance had been jealous once or twice before but never like that. Never to the point where he wanted to punch someone's lights out. He told himself it was because she was his responsibility. Her life was literally in his hands.

Suddenly, he wasn't sure this job had been a good choice. Maybe he was too raw from the experience with Logan and should have just taken some downtime.

Too late now.

"Chance, what were you hoping to do on your vacation while you are here?"

He was vaguely aware someone had spoken to him,

the background of chatter and breakfast falling away as he'd been caught up in his thoughts.

When he snapped to, he realized all eyes were on him.

"I'm sorry," he said, shaking his head. "What was that?"

"I was just wondering what you were hoping to do, if you needed any suggestions, for what there is to do here while you are visiting," Marco said.

"Oh. Well, I thought I would find some beaches, maybe do some diving, if there are opportunities for that. Maybe spend some time in the jungle—I've never had a chance to do that as much as I'd like to."

Not for fun, anyway. He'd been on protective duty in Ecuador once, guarding a politician's family from an assassination attempt, and that had been dicey. Not exactly a relaxed way to enjoy the local flora and fauna.

"I could take you out, for a tour, perhaps, or some hunting," Marco said.

Chance tried to find the best way to decline; he didn't intend on leaving Ana's side, and he certainly wasn't going out into the jungle with Marco.

"We'll see. Today, I think I might just—"

"I know of a good swimming and diving spot nearby, if you are interested," Ana interrupted, saving him. "We can go there. And then there is the holiday to prepare for."

"That sounds great. What do you do for your holiday?"

"Much the same as most countries—parties, food, fireworks to bring in the New Year."

"Though some of the old traditions are fun, too," Lucia said, smiling. At Marco.

Until Lucia caught herself and then looked away.

Chance didn't know if anyone else had caught her expression, but he had.

Huh.

"Like what?" Chance asked.

"It's very festive here. New Year's is like the start of the holiday week, instead of the end. Most do not open their gifts from Christmas and celebrate until Epiphany on January sixth. The party here includes the entire village—everyone meets in the main street, and we celebrate and fireworks are set off over the water. But there are small local and family traditions, as well. Like finding the coin in the *pan dulce* or wearing undergarments in the color that reflects what you would like to happen in the New Year," Ana explained with a grin.

"Excuse me—you mean, underwear?"

Everyone laughed, and Chance wasn't sure he'd heard right. *"Sí,"* Doncia confirmed. "If you need money, for instance, you could wear green boxers, or if you want love and passion, something red. Or you may eat, or be fed by a lover, twelve grapes. One for every month of the New Year, sweet grapes being a good sign, sour ones, well, not so good. But all of our grapes are sweet here," she promised with a smile.

Chance chuckled. "Wow. At home, we usually get some beer, pizza and wings, and all watch the New York City ball drop, then watch movies all night. That's about it."

"Some people also have ceremonial fires and burn old objects or paper they write certain things on, or they throw buckets of water out of their windows for renewal, a kind of symbolic tossing out. Sometimes they wait for passersby, just for fun," Lucia added, again looking at Marco, laughing. "Remember that time…"

Marco and Ana laughed, too, as they all reminisced

about some previous New Year's celebrations. Chance back, listening and enjoying Ana's laugh.

As they all chatted, he could only wonder what color underwear Ana might wear New Year's Eve and if he would get to find out.

# 8

LUCIA PEREZ WAS BOTH ELATED and utterly miserable as she watched Marco talk to her mother, smiling, delivering a kiss on her forehead before leaving the kitchen. He was so handsome that her heart hurt just by looking at him.

His lips had been on hers last night, and it felt as if she had dreamed the entire night. Marco hadn't taken Ana's rejection well, and Lucia had sat and consoled him. Then she had consoled him further, up in her room. He'd been gone when she woke up and hadn't so much as shared a glance with her that indicated he was thinking about what had happened between them the night before.

Maybe she had dreamed it. But no. She still felt the wonderful ache in her limbs and in between her thighs that came with being made love to by a powerful man like Marco.

She treasured it. Lucia had loved him since she was a girl—sixteen to Ana's twelve, she'd been heartbroken when her father had engaged Ana to him, and then again when she'd made a pass at Marco a few years later, throwing caution to the wind.

He'd rejected her, and she'd left to work in the jungles and small villages of Central America.

She thought when she'd come home that it would have gone away, that she would have grown out of her desire for Marco.

But she'd been relieved when Ana said she wasn't marrying him, and thrilled by his response to her last night.

Pushing up from the table, she couldn't just let him leave. She wanted to see his face in the daylight, to acknowledge what had happened between them, at least for a moment, before he left.

"Marco, wait," she called from the doorway, catching him before he reached his truck.

He did wait, but she saw his back stiffen, and he turned around, but looked so serious.

"You left this morning without so much as a goodbye," she said softly, reaching out to touch his chest lightly with her forefinger. He stepped back slightly, looking past her shoulder.

"Lucia, someone might wonder," he cautioned, and she laughed forcefully to cover the pain his withdrawl caused.

"Wonder at what? Two old friends talking?" she asked but was unable to keep the edge from her tone.

"Lucia, last night…"

"I know," she said, looking down to garner the courage. "I'm not a fool. I know you only came to me because you were hurt by Ana, and I know you want her and not me."

"It's not that. I did want you, in case you couldn't tell," he said, his face warming, if only slightly.

Just enough to give her hope.

"I didn't care if you were thinking of her," Lucia said, her cheeks burning at the admission. "Maybe in time, you could grow to love me."

The question hung between them, and Marco blew out a breath.

"Lucia, I don't love Ana, and I wasn't hurt by her. I was...upset because I need to be here. Stay close. And her rejection makes that impossible," he said, dragging a hand over his face, sounding as if every word was being torn from him. "As for learning to love you, I think that's a lesson that would come easily. But this is not the time, not the place. I'm not sure there ever will be, either."

Lucia shook her head. "What are you talking about? You're not making any sense. I don't understand. Wouldn't your family be as happy to have me as her? Is that your worry?"

His eyes burned down into hers, and for one unguarded moment, she saw the desire in his face, the unvarnished need. For her.

Her heart couldn't take it.

"Tell your mother you're going to the store, and I will give you a ride," he said.

Still confused, she nodded, willing to go anywhere with him. She ran to the house, moving quickly, afraid that he might actually leave before she returned. But no, he waited, sitting in his truck as she climbed up beside him.

"What's that?" he asked, looking at the paper she held.

"She gave me a list," Lucia said, smiling. "So I guess I really do need to go to the store. But why did you want me to tell her that?"

"I need to talk to you where no one else will hear us," he said mysteriously as the truck rumbled down the main road, then he took a quick left down an old jungle trail that she knew led to a deserted beach. They'd often played there as children. It was too off the beaten path for tourists, and no one would be there at this time of the morning.

Coming to a break in the trees, the crystal green-blue waters stretched out before them, and Marco cut the engine.

"Let's walk."

Sliding from the truck, Lucia fell into step at his side, taking in the beautiful view. She'd seen many like it through her entire life, but she never tired of it. She'd visited Ana once, in the States, and it was exciting, but she had been happy to come back to Mexico. This was her home.

"Marco, what is this all about?"

Away from the truck, shaded by tall palms and rain-forest trees, Marco didn't say a word but pulled her into his arms and captured her mouth with a passion that left her breathless.

When he pulled away, he had her face framed in his hands, his eyes steady on hers, though his voice trembled slightly, as moved by the passion between them as she was.

"Do you remember when you came to me when you were eighteen? When you wanted me to make love to you? To be your first?"

Her face burned under his hands, and she nodded. She wanted to look away, that rejection still smarting, but he held her fast.

"I wanted nothing more. I wanted to take you that night and make you mine for the nights afterward.

When you left…it was good, and it was terrible," he said.

The words shocked her, and thrilled her. And confused her.

"Then why… I don't understand," Lucia said, pulling away, unsure how to read all of the mixed messages he was sending her way. Was he just trying to make her believe that all of these years he had really wanted her?

"At the time, I was young, too, and I took my family's promise seriously. I felt like I could not be with you without shaming them," he said, shaking his head. "Such outdated, old customs. Even my grandfather laughs about it now, though it's not really funny, because it cost me you."

Lucia looked at him, stunned. "Wait—Marco, what are you saying? That your grandfather no longer holds you to your father's promise? So why all of this, last night, with Ana, your message?"

He took a deep breath, looked out to sea, away from her. Lucia's heart thudded hard in her chest.

"I had no intention of marrying Ana. But…I needed to be around her, to stay close. Closer than a friend of the family would be allowed to stay."

"Why?"

His face changed, becoming serious, the light in his eyes flattening in a way that sent a shiver down her spine.

"No one knows this, *cara.* If I tell you, you literally would hold my life in your hands, and this puts you in danger, as well."

"Tell me, Marco."

"When you left, back then, I thought it would be easier, but it wasn't. So I had to leave, too. I joined the local police, as you know," he said.

"And then quit when you went back to helping your family with the farm and the store."

"In a way. I quit because I was asked to join *los federales* and to work undercover."

Her brow furrowed deeply. "You worked for the PF?"

There had never been a word about Marco working for *policias federales*. Of course, Lucia hadn't been home much and didn't always know what was happening here.

"I work for them now. In fact, I have worked for them since I turned twenty-six. Seven long years of lying to everyone I know, since my work has always been undercover, unknown to anyone but my team and a few in the organization who monitor us and our assignments. We infiltrate cartels, local crime organizations, set up business arrangements with them, gather information. Every now and then, we get to take one of them down."

Lucia's mind spun. How was it possible Marco had managed to have everyone think he simply managed his family business, when he was really an undercover agent?

"No one knows, Lucia. No one. Just you now, and that's breaking every rule I live by, but I couldn't let you think that last night I was just using you. It was… impossible for me to say no to the woman I had dreamed about for years."

"Okay," she said, trying to process everything he was saying, but falling short. "But what does this have to do with Ana?"

"There have been some specific threats against her."

Lucia nodded. "Kidnapping? But they have done that ever since she has become famous. Nothing comes of it."

"This is different. She's funneled so much money

into the villages, funded the efforts to help local people undermine the organization's influence in the local villages—and her wealth is growing. She's inspired people, and they can't allow that. Many of these villages block the paths to the coast, to the shipping routes. They think she's a danger. The threat is real, and it's worse than kidnapping."

Lucia felt her stomach sink, her romantic worries set aside for now. "Ana is in serious danger?"

"As serious as it gets. They don't want to kidnap her—they want her dead. I don't know that her pretty bodyguard is up to the task of keeping her safe," he said, frowning. "I need to get close to her and stay that way until we can find out who it is and eliminate the threat. And get her back in the States."

"Bodyguard? Who?" Had she stepped through the looking glass? Nothing was real or clear anymore.

"Chance. He's not a friend from the States. Ana's TV bosses were countering a threat there, as well. Someone was harassing Ana, and Berringer was hired to watch over her until she's back to work. He's adequate—he and his brothers have a good reputation—but he's one man, and he has no idea of what he's up against. He's also distracted. He just let me walk out of the airport with her, and then, from his reaction to my overtures, I can only think that they are lovers, as well. He lost his temper with me, and that exposes both of them."

"Chance is a bodyguard," Lucia repeated under her breath, absorbing it all. "I can't believe this. So you were willing to lead Ana along, that you would marry her, to remain near her so that you could protect her?"

Marco nodded. "You have to understand, *corazon,* I've done unsavory things in the course of my assignments. Many things that would make you realize I'm not the honorable man you think I am. I would have done whatever I needed to in order protect Ana, to make sure no one got to her."

Lucia understood exactly what he was saying—he would have slept with her sister, as well as promising to marry her, and anything else he needed to do. God knew what else he had done. They all knew the stories, and she'd seen up close what corruption and drug running had done to their country. Lucia knew it was a war, and the men and women fighting that war were asked, sometimes, to do anything, including laying their lives on the line.

Marco was one of them. Like her, fighting to save their country, though in a different way. Her heart swelled with respect, admiration and more love than she would have thought possible.

"Oh, Marco," she said, holding him close. "You are the man I always thought you were, and more."

He stiffened in her embrace and then seemed to collapse into her, his arms coming around her with bruising intensity, burying his face in her hair.

"You are so beautiful. Perfect," he said against her neck, making her soar with need. "You know I kept tabs on you, too, as much as I could. Made sure that you were out of the path of danger. I knew what happened in Cartegena, and it scared the life out of me," he whispered as he kissed her lips, her jaw. "You cannot go back there."

Lucia thrilled that he cared, that he had watched over her through the years. She was also deeply sad—how much they had wasted.

Now was the time to make up for it, she thought, catching his lips with her own, teasing his tongue and drawing him deeper into her. For several long moments, all that existed were their hands, mouths and the sound of the waves crashing around them.

"Marco, let me help," she said against his lips.

"What do you mean?"

"You need to stay close to Ana, but she is with Chance. So…use me. Tell them I have accepted your proposal, and by being engaged to me, you can stay closer to her. And I can keep an eye out, as well, let you know if anything happens or is not right."

Marco grimaced. "No. Just telling you what I have jeopardizes you. I will not do that anymore. You cannot tell anyone what you know, and I cannot use you to do my job. I just…cannot," he said, his eyes on her, revealing the depth of his conflict.

"You can," she said, feeling solid and sure. More so than she had in a while. "Ana is my sister. I want her safe. And I want to be with you. This can work."

"You don't understand, Lucia. When this is over, when Ana is safe and she returns to the States, I will go back to my work. I work with very dangerous people. I cannot afford to ever have them know about the people I love. They would use any of you to get to me, and that means I cannot be with you. Not the way I would want to. Maybe someday, but not now. Maybe not ever."

Lucia felt his pain as her own, and while it hurt, what he was saying, knowing he felt it, too, made it more tolerable.

"I understand, Marco. But if we can have just this, now, this fantasy, why not? It will hurt to part later, but it will hurt to part now, too. And then, maybe someday, when you are done with your work… I will wait for you."

The raw emotion in his face nearly made her knees give out, but Lucia meant every word that she said. She wanted to be with Marco more than she wanted her next breath. If she could have him now, and help keep her sister safe in the process, then she could live with whatever came later.

"If you are sure, Lucia. If you are sure," he said, weakening, his hands on her, slipping under the material of her loose shift, making her heart slam against her ribs, her bones melt with wanting.

"I've never been so sure of anything in my life," she said, giving herself up to him and losing herself in their embrace since it was likely all that they would have.

ANA WAS HAPPY TO GET AWAY from the house. She lifted her face to the sunshine filtering down through the thick vegetation as she paused to take in the sky. The spot where she was leading Chance had to be approached on foot, and they'd left his Jeep back near the road.

"I love this," she said on a sigh, reaching out to touch a vibrant, hot-pink bloom at the end of a bushy plant. "I've forgotten, especially in recent years, how fecund everything is here. How dense and lovely."

A cool bit of air reached them through the trees. The coast was less than a mile away, and Ana had a very special treat for Chance. She knew it would appeal to his adventurous spirit.

"It is gorgeous. I've spent some time in the jungles farther south, in Argentina and Brazil, but not as much here. This is different," he observed.

"You'll love where we're going. The entire Yucatán has rugged landscapes, more so than you might guess from the cities and villages. There are a lot of surprises in the jungles and along the coast," she said, wanting to entice him.

And wanting to be alone with him. The place they

were going would be secluded—special and used only by locals—not swarmed with holiday tourists.

"I've read a bit about it. About cenotes, in particular. And caves. I wouldn't have thought there would be so many caves, but I suppose it makes sense, given the water surrounding the peninsula and the areas. Like Florida, with all of the sinkholes."

"Except that ancient Mayan civilizations often were located on ours," she said with a smile. "And people tend not to build their houses on them."

Chance laughed. "So where are you taking me? To a famous cenote?"

"You'll see," Ana said mischievously. "Catch me if you can," she added and took off running.

Chance was startled for a second, and she laughed as she heard him yell her name behind her, but she knew these paths and lands like the back of her hand, even after all of these years. The jungle, the ocean... they were still in her blood, and her pulse raced as she sped away, looking back to see Chance in close pursuit.

She was almost there, and for fun, she ducked behind the thick trunk of a wide old mahogany tree. Ana held her breath, staying still as she heard Chance approach and then stop.

"Ana?"

She heard him step forward, slowly, cautiously. He was only feet from where she hid.

"Ana?"

This time his voice was more worried, and he walked faster.

Ana jumped out in front of him, making a face and a noise as she did so, and laughed hysterically as he jumped back, completely taken off guard.

As she laughed, he regarded her with his hands on

his hips, trying to look stern. She could see, however, that he was having a difficult time of it.

"Not funny, Ana. I thought you might have been hurt or lost. Or something bad."

She shook her head, still laughing. "Oh, please. Lost? I played in these jungles when I was a girl. You would be the one to get lost, not me," she charged, catching her breath. "You should have seen your face. Did you think I was something dangerous? A wildcat? A jaguar?" She teased, making a purring noise low in her throat that finally cracked him up.

They both stood laughing for a few more minutes and then stopped. Chance came forward, drawing her into his arms.

"It's not often someone can surprise me, but you seem to do it every other moment," he said, kissing the top of her head in an endearing way that made her gasp. Passion, she understood with him; but affection, that hit a different note in her heart.

"I have more surprises for you," she said, tilting her face up and planting a light kiss on his lips. "Come on, you'll see," she said, grasping his hand and pulling him forward.

He let her tug him along, and minutes later, as they found themselves standing on the edge of a high bluff, she heard his whispered exclamation as he looked out over the view.

"This is amazing. It's like a…like another world."

She felt a surge of pleasure at his response and the excited light in his eyes.

"This is a sacred place to our village. Our ancestors worshipped and conducted much of their ceremonial life among these ruins," she explained. "Once, it was a place we came as children to play and explore, but now, as we grow older, it's also a way of connecting with our past. Real people who shared our bloodlines lived here. It still leaves me in awe to think that they built all of this, even when only these broken parts remain," she said reverently.

Chance put his hands on her shoulders as they stood taking it in. A lush waterfall burst through the jungle on the other side of the glen, pouring down into a dark green pool formed by the cenote. It was surrounded by steep walls and worn-down ruins blanketed by lush vegetation.

"Can we get down there?" he asked. "Or do we just look from here?"

"We can definitely go. We can walk around to the other side and take the steps down through the ruins. Or...there is one more way," she said, turning to him.

He seemed to tower over her out here, big and masculine, looking as wild as the landscape around him. He wasn't native, but somehow, she thought, he fit.

"What's the other way?"

She smiled, stepping back and slipping her shirt over her head, then undoing the button of her jeans. She wore her bathing suit underneath but felt his eyes move over her as hungrily as if she didn't.

"Ana? What's the other way down?"

Her grin widened. "We dive. Or jump. Your choice."

Chance peered down over the side. "That has to be about thirty feet."

"Twenty-eight or so. The water is deep, and there are no rocks. We've dived from this spot ever since we were young. Used to start back there—" she pointed to the tree where she had hidden "—and run and fly off the side. It was magical, flying through the air and then down into that water," she said.

Chance was already peeling his shirt off. "You said we might go diving, but I thought you meant more like scuba," he said, revealing that he had worn a pair of trunks, as well.

"Are you afraid of the jump?" she asked innocently but had to smother a grin.

He sent her a "get real" look. "I dived from plat-forms twice this height or higher, I'll have you know, in Acapulco."

"Impressive," she said, though she wasn't completely commenting on his diving experience.

He was wearing tight, short black trunks that hid very little, including the fact that he was somewhat ex-cited. Ana couldn't help but look. In the light of day, so close to her, he was even more magnificent.

"Let's jump," she suggested, her tone a bit more husky. "Together. We can dive later."

Chance reached out, took her hand, and they both walked back about eight feet or so and paused, looking at each other with a big smile.

"Now!" Ana yelled, and they rushed forward to-gether, leaping out into the air and splashing into the cool water seconds later.

Ana let go of Chance's hand under the surface of the water and came to the top gasping.

"It's colder than I remember," she said, laughing.

He swam up close, wrapping his arms around her, and her legs around his hips.

"Let me warm you up."

Their bodies pressed close, her breasts crushed against his chest in the most delightful way as he kissed her, and she twined her arms around his shoulders.

It was like being in another world, one that left ev-erything else behind, even time itself. Ana lost herself in the kiss, in touching Chance, and forgot to worry about anything as his tongue rubbed along hers, his hands on her back, massaging, cupping her backside and pressing her against his hardness.

"Chance, you tempt me, but there's so much more here," she said, wanting him, but wanting to share this place with him even more. There was time for the rest. "And more private places," she added.

"I like the sound of that. Lead on."

Ana smiled, floating back out of his arms, beckoning him to come with her, as if she were some kind of sea nymph.

She'd been here often and always visited when she was home, but as she watched Chance's powerful arms cut through the water as he swam after her, no other moment in her life compared. Ana had the scary suspicion that after knowing Chance Berringer, no other man would compare, either.

# 9

CHANCE WAS INTRIGUED, and here, in this sacred spot so far away from the rest of the world—or so it seemed—he let himself think only of this time and the woman he was with.

Ana led him behind the waterfall into a room that was carved in the rock—not a cave, but an actual cavern that was part of the ruin built above. The waterfall crashed outside the entrance, barring any view inside. Ana pulled herself up gracefully from the water onto the stone platform, worn smooth by time and water. Chance followed.

"This is incredible," he said, feeling as if he was repeating himself, but he couldn't help being wowed by this spot. He'd seen ruins before, had climbed through Machu Picchu, even, but this was even more special. Maybe because he was here with Ana, and it was a glimpse into her world, her past. He loved the look of reverence and joy on her face—the only other time he had seen her as happy was when she was cooking on her old TV show. And when he was inside of her.

The trunks he wore were a tad uncomfortable given

his sort of perpetually aroused state. The cool water had helped some, but there was no doubt that he wanted Ana again, as soon as he could have her.

"Follow me," she called and headed deeper into the recesses of the cave.

"Anywhere," Chance murmured with a smile and set off after her.

They entered a wide, much lower tunnel that seemed to squeeze the light from the spot where they had emerged, and for a moment, Chance wondered if this was safe. But Ana walked ahead at a steady, confident rate, obviously knowing where she was going.

It got very dark before they turned a corner toward light again and emerged in a smaller cave that was lit only with dappled sunshine from far above. There were markings on the walls, and ornate statues and carvings surrounded the area, almost like unfound treasure.

"What is this?" he asked.

Ana knelt by the side of the rock shelf, dipped her hand down and scooped up a handful of mud.

Chance smiled. "I've heard of this. Terra-cotta mud pools."

"Mud baths, yes. This one is used only by the people of our village, guarded closely, as it is believed to have healing and even magical properties."

"What are all the carvings and the markings?"

"Some are millennia old. Some are from last week, offered at the seasonal changes, connections to the old ones, ancestors and gods. Many people in our village still follow old ways."

Chance nodded. "Is it okay for me to be here?"

Ana laughed lightly. "Of course. You are with me, and I wanted to share this with you. And on a workday, no one else is likely to come by. Evenings, more people will come, and weekends."

Chance watched as she reached behind her, undoing the strap that held the top of her bathing suit on. He sucked in a breath as the scrap of bright blue fell to the ground, and Ana stood there mostly naked before him.

She was like one of the ancient goddesses, he thought, with her dark hair and fiery eyes, and that magnificent body. Lush curves contrasted with firm muscle, and her full breasts pouted at him, nipples hard and dark.

Ana didn't break eye contact as she slid her bottoms off, too, and Chance was mesmerized. He'd had women do much more elaborate stripteases for him, but he couldn't recall anything sexier than Ana taking off her bathing suit.

"Your turn," she said with a mischievous smile.

Chance wasted no time shucking his trunks and followed as she sat on the side of the rock and dipped her legs into the mud.

"It's good to ease inside, take your time. It's very warm, though it won't burn. But it can be a lot if you aren't used to it," she explained.

"How deep is it?" he asked, sliding one foot in, then the other, and finding the thick mud to be pleasantly soft, not slimy, and nicely warm in the coolness of the cave.

"Only waist deep. When you feel ready, you can go all the way in, and it's all one depth. On that end, there are ledges carved from the rock where you can stretch out."

"Luxurious," he commented, slowly lowering into the warm mud, making sure sensitive spots were okay with taking the plunge.

But once he was in, he sighed. "This is wonderful.

I've heard people rave about mud baths, and always thought it was some kind of silly spa thing."

"The earth is sacred to my people, and even now, the baths are supposed to have healing effects. Elders use the mud in some rituals and in medicines. Not ones recognized by some people, of course," she said, moving slowly to the far side, where she stretched out on one of the ledges, up to her shoulders in mud.

Chance missed the view of her luscious body but went with her, enjoying the way his muscles were loosening, his mind lulled by the warmth and the weight of the mud. It was almost hypnotizing, and he commented as much as he slid up onto the ledge next to Ana, also sliding down so that he was mostly covered.

He lay there, covered in ancient mud, deep in the earth, surrounded by Mayan carvings, markings, and took it all in. Looking up, he stared at what had to be a seventy-foot drop from the jungle floor to this spot.

"Seems dangerous—do people, animals, fall in?"

She shook her head. "There is a brick wall, like a well, that protects the opening and bans anyone from entering. Through the waterfall is the only access. If someone looks down from above, all they see is dark. Very forbidding."

"I bet. So no one can see us down here?"

"No."

Chance was shaken from his ruminations when he felt Ana's hand slide along his thigh, a strange sensation in the warm mud, and even more so when she found his cock and closed her hand over him.

"Ana." He sighed, letting his head fall back as she stroked him to hardness, the warmth and the slippery sensations of her skin and the silky mud creating a sensual combination that had him ready to explode in seconds. "Stop, or I'm going to…" he said, his breath coming short.

"Okay, we should wait until we wash the mud off," she agreed, taking her hand from him and coming up along next to him, laying her head on his shoulder.

"Mmm-hmm." He turned his head, finding her mouth and kissing her in deep, drugging kisses as his fingers did to her breasts what she had done to him under the surface. She whimpered into his mouth, arching against him.

"Maybe time to go wash off now?" he suggested, and she nodded eagerly.

They grabbed their suits and made their way gingerly back to the falls, laughing as they stopped to kiss, caress and stroke each other to an even higher level of arousal. Their muddy bodies stuck together, creating noises that collapsed them in laughter as well as turning them on.

Peeping out from the fall to make sure they were still alone, Chance waved to her to join him, and once more, they plunged into the cool water.

"Wow, I've never felt anything like this," Chance said as he dived under, washing the mud from his body, invigorated and feeling a vibration of energy that he'd never quite experienced before. He was also achingly hard—not even the cool water could ease that after all of the foreplay.

Ana was floating on her back, her breasts bobbing up from the water, her face serene. But when she turned her face to look at him, he saw the same raw desire in her eyes.

"Now" was all he said, and she nodded, swimming back to the fall, to the privacy it provided.

Chance didn't want to play any more when he took

her in his arms again, too hungry and too desperate for her to wait any longer. But...

"Damn." He bit out a curse. "I left any protection I have back in the truck."

Ana's hand stroked him lightly as she kissed him.

"I told you, I'm safe. Protected. I assume you are healthy," she said, biting his neck. "I don't want to wait, Chance."

"Yes," he said roughly, sitting down on the cool rock and pulling her onto his lap, facing him.

Her legs wrapped around his hips as she sat, taking him deep in one motion, making them both shudder with the sheer intensity of it.

She looked at him with sooty eyes, smudged with need as she sat facing him, his cock buried deep inside.

"I told you I couldn't wait," she said before she kissed him.

Chance was lost. Her nails dug into his shoulders, and he grabbed her bottom, moving her on him in short, tight moves that had him at the edge, but he needed more.

"Ana, I've never needed anyone like this, like you," he said, feeling vulnerable at the admission but needing to share it.

"I know. It's how I feel with you, too. Nothing has ever been like this. Only with you," she said softly, making his heart beat even harder. He could see the truth in her eyes.

What was happening between them? More than sex, he thought. More than the job. He worried about Ana where he had never really done that with previous clients. He wanted her, but want had developed into something stronger—he needed her. That was something he had never quite felt before, with anyone.

"Come here," she said, leading him over to the smooth wall of the inside of the cave. She faced the wall, planted her hands and looked back over her shoulder at him. She was temptation itself.

But as much as Chance was happy to give her anything she wanted—anything she desired—he wanted her close this time. He wanted to feel her heat, her breath on his skin, and be able to see her as they made love.

Love? No, he thought. Just an expression, but still... Now was not the time for thinking so much, so he turned her back around to face him. He could give them both what they wanted, and pulled her up, close to him, face-to-face, and pressed her into the cool rock wall.

She sighed in happiness, smiling, and he smiled back.

Taking her hips in his hands, he surged into her, their sighs and moans mingling as the connection between them eased some of the ache. But it wasn't nearly enough.

He moved, and her nails dug into his shoulders as he kissed her, losing himself in everything that was Ana. He was close and snuck a hand down between them.

"So ready, so hot," he panted, stroking her clit to the rhythm of his thrusts. "Come with me, Ana, please," he almost begged, knowing he wouldn't last much longer.

Everything primal and masculine within him was let loose, feeling her tense, how her inner muscles gripped him and then loosened, bathing him in hot honey as she came and came, her head falling forward as she chanted his name.

He took hold of her hips with both hands again, pressing deep, watching the beautiful arch of her back, the slope of her neck when his body finally released into hers, the climax so strong he was left shaking from it.

"Damn, Ana. I can't feel my legs," he said, half laughing but sliding down the wall to the cool floor, taking her with him.

"It's the mud."

"No, I don't think so."

It was her. She astounded him in ways he'd never imagined a woman could. And it was more than the sex, though the sex was outstanding. Her sense of mystery, adventure, and her love for her work and her family shone through her. Her adamant independence and the passion that she threw into everything she did.

Most of the women he dated were the ones who watched when he did something daring, but he had a feeling Ana would be the kind to jump in right beside him, like she did at the cliff.

"This is nice." She sighed. "Being away from everything, everyone. Leaving it all back there."

Chance murmured his agreement. It was nice. To be with Ana and not have to worry or be on guard, to have a moment just to enjoy her.

It was also dangerous. He wanted more, but if his attention was on her, he could miss something else. Like something that could bring her harm.

Suddenly, he had new respect for the conflicts his brothers must have dealt with when they had been protecting women they loved.

Not that Chance was in love. He wasn't even sure he'd know it if he was.

"We should head back," she said. "I told Mama I would help her with party preparations later today, and after this, I think I need a nap first." She yawned. "I can't remember the last time I took a nap. Never any time back in New York."

"Success has its price," Chance joked, offering her

his hand as he pulled her up from sitting. Between the mud bath and the sex, his muscles were loose and warm, and he wanted to extend this just a little longer.

"Let's take a swim first? Just a quick one, and then we can go," he said.

"Sure," she agreed and reached for her suit.

"Maybe we can leave that here."

"But…someone might see. People do come to this spot," she said.

He smiled. "That's what makes it so fun. But no one will see us beneath the water. C'mon," he urged, holding out his hand.

Ana took it, and they ran out from the cover of the falls and straight into the water, laughing like a couple of kids. For all of the excitement Chance experienced on a regular basis, he'd forgotten what it was like just to act like a kid again.

Splashing and diving, they played like a couple of sea otters for a few minutes, until Chance swam down deep, coming up from under where she treaded water, and grabbed her leg, pulling her down, too.

Ana's eyes were wide with surprise when they met his, and he captured her mouth under the surface for a hot kiss. He couldn't get enough of how she captivated him. She kissed with her whole body, putting everything she was into it.

Something popped by his ear, and Chance didn't think anything of it at first, but then it happened again, and he felt Ana jerk away from him.

Opening his eyes, there was a crimson ribbon floating in the water, and his heart slammed in his chest as several more pops—bullets—broke the surface of the water.

And Ana, drifting away from him in the clear blue water, was bleeding.

ANA WASN'T SURE WHAT was happening.

She'd been diving into the most delicious underwater kiss with Chance when something tore at her arm, making her jerk back.

She thought something had attacked her, biting her. A wild animal of some sort or some biting fish, but the sight of her own blood streaming into the water had erased her thoughts and panic overtook her.

As they both surfaced, sucking in air, Ana found herself pushed back down, under the water and under Chance as he forced her to go deeper, beneath him as he dragged her toward the falls.

She must have passed out because the next thing she knew she was flat on her back on the stone floor, naked and shivering.

She'd been so warm before, and now she was freezing. Where was Chance?

She pushed herself up, looking for him, and saw he was crouched over by the edge of the falls, peering out. Looking down, she saw her shoulder had been wrapped—his bathing suit—and ached like the devil. In fact, it felt as if her arm was going to fall off.

"Chance?" she said, coughing water. She was surprised to hear her voice so weak.

He turned, rushing to her side. "You're okay. It's just a scratch, though I know it doesn't feel like one."

His eyes were all over her, searching her face, every feature in his expression tight and strained.

"A scratch? From what?"

"From a bullet. We're lucky nothing worse, but they're still out there. Can you walk?"

"I don't know. I think so," she said. "Someone shot at us?"

"Seems so. They have the ruins covered and you

said the only exit is above the mud bath. But is there any other path out?"

"There used to be some passages up underneath the jungle, under the ruins of the steps, but they aren't easily accessible."

Ana was still trying to understand why someone had been shooting at them, her head reeling from the pain in her arm.

"Is there a place you can hide?" he asked.

She thought and nodded. "Yes, but what are you going to do? You can't take them on, unarmed and…" She looked at him, completely naked. It didn't seem to bother him at all. If anything, it made him more fierce; a pure male animal.

A shiver went down her spine.

"There isn't much choice. My clothes are up on the cliff where we jumped. And my phone is in my jeans," he said, swearing at himself under his breath. "Tell me how to make it back out."

"You can access the caves to the jungle from the other side of the mud baths," she explained as he helped her to her feet, making sure she was steady before he let go. When he did, she missed the warmth of his body, the strength of his hands. But she could stand on her own, and she did.

"You find a place to hide, stay there, stay quiet. I'll be back to get you." He leaned in, kissed her quickly and walked off. For the first time in a long time, Ana was completely afraid. She wanted to go with him or for him to come back. What if something terrible happened to him? There were men with guns out there.

The shooters wouldn't come through the waterfall— they'd have to swim to do that—but they would take the caves, which was where Chance was heading. It was the only other route out—there was no way to scale the cliffs on the sides of the cenote.

Her legs were feeling stronger by the minute, and adrenaline was chasing away the throbbing in her shoulder. Peeling away the material, she saw the deep scour in her skin had stopped bleeding, mostly.

Infection, especially here, would be an issue, but not for the moment.

Sliding on her bathing suit, she grabbed Chance's as well and turned to follow him. She couldn't let him face this alone, and maybe she could help. There had to be more than one of them, and if something happened to him, whoever was after them would just be coming for her next, anyway.

Padding along quickly, she searched for him in the dim light of the cave and finally saw a shadow up ahead. It had to be Chance.

Hurrying to join him, she tried to get his attention. "Chance? Chance!"

The figure turned and paused, then came back in her direction.

She walked forward to meet him halfway, then froze as the silhouette became larger, and she realized this was not Chance. Too beefy, too short.

And carrying a gun.

Ana froze.

"Don't run, *chica*. I can just shoot you in the back, then," the man said in Spanish, making her blood run cold.

"Where's Chance?"

"Your lover? I don't know. One of the other men has killed him, most likely."

As her pursuer broke into a dim bit of light, she held her breath at the sheer cruelty in his face.

"But you…you are mine. Maybe for a while. No need to kill you right away, as long as the job is done sooner or later."

A peep of sheer fear escaped her lips, and Ana felt her eyes burn with tears, but she couldn't lose it now. She had to force herself to think. Chance could be hurt or dead, and she was on her own to survive this.

"I'd rather you shot me," she spat and ran away toward the waterfall.

His laugh followed her down through the caves.

If she made it to the falls, she could get in the water and hide there. He didn't look like much of a swimmer.

She stumbled, her foot hitting something sharp, and she cried out but picked up and kept running, his laugh following her.

Why would someone want to kill her? There was no way this guy was her stalker. Then again, random violence happened in the jungles all the time—drug runners could think that she and Chance had seen something they shouldn't have, and that was all it might take.

The light of the opening where the water fell was only yards ahead, and she picked up the pace. So did her attacker, his heavy footsteps breaking into a run. He'd figured out what she was aiming for.

But then, suddenly, the footsteps stopped, and Ana stood at the edge of the waterfall, daring a look behind her.

Nothing.

Hugging the side of the opening in case she had to jump, she felt a trickle down her arm and saw that her wound had started bleeding again.

Shot. She still couldn't get her mind around it.

Then a shadow emerged, and she stifled a scream,

poised to jump into the water. She'd have to dive under the crash of the falls. There was no other option.

A hard hand jerked her back, and she screamed, turning to find it wasn't her attacker.

"Chance!" she sobbed, shaking from head to foot.

"Ana, what were you thinking? I told you to hide," he said, pulling her in, holding her tight, until the shaking stopped.

"What h-happened? H-he said you were dead," she said, trying to get steady again.

"There were only the two. I took out the one ahead of him and was waiting on this one when you burst on the scene," he said, his lips turning downward in disapproval. "What part of 'stay here and hide' did you miss?"

That sparked her temper, and she was glad for it. "I didn't want to hide. I thought you might need help, and either way, I was just a sitting duck, waiting here. I thought you might need…help."

Chance's eyebrows lifted, and the side of his lips, pressed so sternly together, lifted a bit at the edge. "I guess I should have known that you'd do something like that."

"So you were there all the while?"

He nodded. "I was right behind him, but I had to wait for you to get enough distance, and for him to be completely distracted, before I made my move. I couldn't believe it when you popped up in the cave, calling my name. Please, Ana, please. Don't ever do that again."

The concern, relief and something deeper, in his tone, made the anger leech from her, and she nodded, tucking in against him. She'd been scared to death, sick at the thought of something happening to him—and now she realized he had felt the same about her, when she had appeared in the cave. Because he cared, or because she was his client? Maybe both?

Everything was muddled, her thinking suddenly fuzzy.

"Okay, let's get out of here. These guys are out cold, but we need to get back to our clothes and call the authorities. Can you make it? You're too pale. I can carry you."

"No, I can walk," she said, intending to do so, though if she hadn't been convinced before not to leave Chance's side until they were safe again, she was now. The way his arm was slung around her, holding her close, she assumed he was feeling exactly the same way.

## 10

"I HATE LYING TO THEM," Ana said, wincing as they left the doctor's office, her shoulder bandaged and attended to. They'd called the police, but the men were gone by the time they arrived. Presumably, they'd disappeared into the jungle.

The police took their report, but Chance didn't imagine anything much would come of it. For all he knew, the police could be in bed with whoever had shot at them. It happened.

"I know."

"No, you don't. I have to tell them, at least Mama. She will find out, anyway. The police know, the doctor... News travels here. It's a small place."

Chance leaned forward on the steering wheel, pinching the bridge of his nose. He had a major headache coming on. Ana was right. After something like today, it would be hard to keep his reason for being here a secret. He'd talked with Garrett while Ana was being treated, and predictably, his older brother had advised them to come back to the States, where they could put Ana in hiding until this threat—or the multiple threats—had passed.

It had taken her less than one second to refuse.

His new and unexpected feelings for Ana aside, this situation was becoming untenable, largely because he had no idea what to expect and from whom.

The threat in the States was there, and the kidnapping chatter was a concern, but this wasn't a kidnapping attempt. Someone had been trying to kill them.

To kill Ana. His hands formed into fists at the thought.

Her hand was on his shoulder then. "Chance. Are you okay?"

He took a breath. "Yeah. I'm fine. It's you I'm worried about. We're not sure what we're dealing with here, and that makes it harder to control the threat." He paused, not wanting to coerce her, but what he had to say was also the truth. "And if these people want you, Ana, whoever they are, it could put your family in danger, too, for you to be here. We really should leave. I know it's hard, but—"

"I'm not leaving, Chance. Don't you see? If I leave, it accomplishes nothing. These people could still come after my family to get at me. It's how they work. Believe me, I know. We grew up with such things. It's why I've worked so hard to help build our village, to build the shops, the medical center, to make them secure and independent. So that they could not be so easily preyed upon. Leaving will just make me a coward. I would be running back to the States with you, hiding, and letting my family stay here, clueless as to the danger."

Chance didn't like it, but she had a point, he supposed. He also admired the hell out of her.

"I have to tell them. I have to let them know what

happened, so that they know. It's the only way we can be safe."

Chance wasn't sure he could argue. The village was small, insular. They could watch out for anyone new, strange.

Or, for all they knew, someone there was the danger.

There were no easy answers.

"Okay, we tell your family, but that's all. And, Ana, you have to start listening to me, please. Back at the cave, that guy could have shot you on sight, and there would have been nothing I could do. You have to trust me. I'm trying to keep you safe."

He saw her struggle with what he was telling her. She didn't like being told what to do. She followed her instincts.

But right now, she had to trust his.

She nodded. "Okay. Yes. I will. I promise," she said softly.

"I guess there's not much way for us to hide what happened today, anyway. We look like we just crawled out of a jungle brawl," he said, smiling to lighten the mood. "How's your arm?"

"Fine. The painkillers work a little too well," she admitted, tilting her head back against the headrest.

"Take a nap while we drive back. You need it."

She didn't need to be told twice, snoozing quietly almost before he was back on the road.

Chance took no chances, sticking to public highways and making sure no one was following them. He'd stuffed away his thoughts and reactions to what happened, focusing only on Ana and getting her to the doctor, talking to the police, but now it all rushed back.

The creep who had held the gun on her, who had threatened to do worse.

Chance took a breath, clearing the red haze that formed in his brain when he thought about it. He needed to set emotions aside.

There was something about that guy, something in the way he had approached Ana. What had he said? That as long as he killed her, he'd done his job, regardless of how long it took, or something to that effect.

That meant it wasn't random violence, as the police suggested. They'd been after Ana specifically. A contract. But why? There was no way this was related to what had happened back in New York.

As Ana mentioned, though, she funneled huge amounts of money into the villages. She'd created wealth and stability among her people and funded several other efforts in the region to provide the kind of safety that drug runners, in particular, would resist. Perhaps Ana was making their lives a little too difficult?

In which case, they wouldn't stop coming for her. She was also right that they would use whatever they could against her, including her family.

Chance clenched his jaw in frustration. He couldn't keep them all safe by himself. If this truly was what was going on, he would need help, or something bad was going to happen. He could feel it in his gut.

Fifteen minutes later, they were back at the house.

It was his bad luck that Ana's mother, Lucia and Marco—always Marco—were standing outside, engaged in an excited conversation. That became even more the case when Chance drove up and Ana's family saw them, dirty, bloody, bandaged.

"*Madre de Dios,* what happened? Did you have an accident?" Doncia exclaimed as she hurried to the car.

Ana had fallen into a deep sleep, no doubt caused

by painkillers as well as exhaustion, and she woke suddenly at her mother's exclamation.

Chance didn't miss how Ana flinched as her mother reached for her, still sluggish from her nap. She was tough. Brave. But the confrontation had frightened her, clearly. He knew that, and it was to be expected. He also knew that she would hate being afraid, more than almost anything.

"What happened?" Marco asked with an accusing look aimed in Chance's direction.

"It's a long story, and Ana's tired. We should get inside, and then we can explain," he said, sliding out of the vehicle and heading around to the other side to help Ana from the Jeep. She leaned gratefully into his side as they walked to the house, unusual for her. That made him worry a little more.

"I will make us some cool tea. It will help," Doncia said, obviously needing to do something helpful.

"That would be great," Chance agreed with a smile.

Chance noted that Marco and Lucia stayed by the Jeep, deep in conversation, not following them immediately. That was fine with him.

Inside, Ana let out a sigh of relief, and so did Chance. He led her to a comfortable lounge in the main room, perfectly positioned to catch the soft breeze circulating from the ceiling fans.

"You okay?" he asked, pushing a lock of silky hair back from her face.

She nodded. "The medicine hit me harder than I thought. I could barely keep my eyes open. But I don't feel anything," she said, her words somewhat slurred as she smiled and raised a hand to his face. "Hmm, except for all the things I feel for you, which are quite nice," she admitted.

Chance told himself it was the drugs talking, though his heart skipped a little at her words. A hopeful skip. Chance pressed his mouth into her palm, holding it there as he kissed it, then dropped it as he heard footsteps behind them.

"Here we are. Fresh iced tea with mango," Doncia said, coming back in with a tray, her tone and smile falsely bright.

"*Gracias,* Mama," Ana said, pushing up to sit straighter on the lounge and taking a sip from the glass her mother gave her.

Marco and Lucia came in, looking serious and suspicious. Chance knew this wasn't going to be an easy conversation. He sat down at the foot of the lounge that Ana occupied and took a sip of his own tea before speaking.

"I might as well cut to the chase," he said, looking them in the eye with a grimace. "We were attacked in the jungle. Ana took me to the cenote, the mud baths, and two men cornered us there and shot at us while we were swimming."

Doncia sucked in a breath, the glass of tea she held tipping in her hand. "My Ana was shot?" she asked, her eyes riveted on Ana's bandages.

Chance reached across, took her glass and put it on the table, and held her cold hand in his. "Scratched. It didn't even need stitches. It's painful, but it will heal easily. There's no need to worry."

Lucia's eyes went wide as she stood, pacing the space between them. "No need to worry? Someone tried to kill my sister, and almost did!"

Chance saw up close that Ana's temper was apparently a family trait.

Chance had to come clean. "It was a close call, but it's my job to make sure nothing happens to Ana, and

I plan to make sure that's the case. I was hired by her production company to watch out for her in New York and to come to Mexico with her just in case. But I don't think this shooting incident has anything to do with the problem back in the States. This is something else altogether. These two men had tracked us to that spot, and they were targeting Ana specifically. The question is, why? There was some talk of a kidnapping threat, but these men didn't want to kidnap Ana. They were clearly guns for hire," Chance said, watching the reactions of Ana's family.

Lucia was markedly not as shocked as Chance would have expected. Doncia had turned a bit more pale, and Marco remained inscrutable.

"What happened to these men?" Marco finally asked.

"I managed to overtake them in the caves and we escaped. But by the time the police arrived, they were gone."

"Thank you, Chance, *gracias,*" Doncia said, squeezing his hand tightly.

"Don't thank me too soon, Doncia. Those men are still out there, and we don't really know why they are after Ana or when they will strike next. The situation has become dangerous for everyone, and that's why I think it would be best if Ana returned to the U.S. immediately."

ANA, LULLED BY THE DRUGS and the conversation, sat up abruptly, shocked by Chance's statement.

"What? No. We already discussed this. Even if I am gone, the threat remains the same. I will not run back to the States like some frightened child and leave my family here to deal with this mess," she said, anger burning off the last of the drug-induced fog.

Her shoulder started throbbing again, but she ignored it.

"Ana, I know—"

"You don't know," she bit off, sending him a furious look. "And you don't get to decide. I am not going back to the States, and that is that," she said definitively, sitting back in her chair.

Chance raised an eyebrow, staring at her. "I have my orders, and so do you. The company execs said that in the case of a direct threat, you were to—"

"They don't run my life and neither do you," Ana insisted and pushed herself up to standing. She swayed slightly, swatting away helpful hands that tried to steady her.

"Ana, be reasonable," Chance tried, but she only glared at him and stalked to the window, staring out.

"You should listen to Chance, Ana. He only wants you to be safe," her mother said sternly, making Ana spin around, looking at her mother in disbelief.

"It does make sense," Lucia chimed in, and Ana's eyes went wide.

"Are you all trying to get rid of me? Why are you taking *his* side?" Ana nearly wailed, becoming undone by the pain in her shoulder, the stress of her day and sheer exhaustion. This was when she needed to be around her family the most, and they were all trying to send her away!

Lucia crossed the room, squeezing her in a hug, and Ana let her, hugging her back and wiping away tears. She hated being so emotional, but she couldn't seem to help it. She'd come here to relax, to get away from everything and to be with her family. But it seemed as if trouble followed her no matter what.

"We're sorry, Ana. We are not taking sides, just trying to do what will keep you safe. You scared us, you know," her sister said, framing Ana's face in her hands.

"But it's New Year's Eve tomorrow," Ana said and shook her head. "I will be safe if I stay here. No one will come into the village, to our home, especially during the holiday. I can go back afterward, but I want to spend the holiday with you all, so much. Please," Ana said, but she was looking over Lucia's shoulder to Chance.

She knew he had her best interests at heart, but she was not leaving. The studio could sue her, and he could leave if he wanted, but she was staying at least through the New Year. She wasn't about to let a bunch of thugs chase her away.

"I suppose it would work," Chance said. "If you stay here. If you go out, I go with you, even if it's just to the store."

Ana nodded.

"Marco will be here, as well as Lucia, and all of our family around for the holiday," Doncia said, looking happier, as well. "Our people take care of their own. We will know if anyone comes around who should not be here. And Ana has taken care of all of us for so long. It is time she let us take care of her," her mother said, nodding resolutely, but her eyes were warm in a way that made Ana's sting with happy tears again.

"Marco, you are staying? Doesn't your family want you home for the holiday?" Ana asked, not wanting to sound ungracious but also not wanting to deal with any more awkwardness, of people assuming they were engaged, et cetera, if Marco was staying in her family home.

Her mother smiled broadly. "Marco is our family, or will be," she said mysteriously.

Ana frowned. "I don't understand—"

Lucia strode to Marco's side, took his hand. "Marco and I are engaged. I know it's sudden, but he's fulfilling his family's promise, Ana. He and I have been in love since we were young. There just has not been any chance, and now, well, there is," she said nervously as they waited for Ana's reaction.

Ana blinked. She was surprised—but also relieved.

"Lucia…Marco, that's wonderful! But why have you waited so long? You shouldn't have let that old arrangement keep you apart when you wanted to be together! I would have happily released you from your promise years ago, Marco," she said, coming forward to embrace them both. "I'm so happy for you," she said, and she meant it.

Lucia looked as if she were glowing, and Ana wondered why she had never seen it before. Now that she knew, she remembered how Lucia and Marco had been when they were younger, always standing together, always talking, always smiling. Marco looked happier, too. But there was still something strained about him, something quiet, that Ana couldn't put her finger on.

"Why did Papa promise me to Marco, when Lucia loved him?"

"He had no idea," Doncia said with a shrug. "And I am sure he would approve of how things have developed. Both of his girls doing so well in life and finding such wonderful men."

Ana met her mother's eyes and then Chance's, but there was no time to deal with that comment as Doncia winked at them both and stood up, clapping her hands together lightly.

"And so we have a party to prepare for tomorrow! So much work to do. Ana, you should go clean up and rest. We will get started."

"I'm fine, Mama. The medicine is wearing off, though I do need a shower. I will stick with taking aspirin. The scratch is not too bad, and those painkillers are too strong. I want to enjoy every minute of being here."

"As we do with you, Ana. Now, go wash up, and I will begin preparing the kitchen so that we can all make tamales!" her mother said joyously.

"We should go, too. Mama had asked us to pick up supplies earlier, but then you came back. We should do that now," Lucia said, but the look she sent Marco made Ana smile. Her sister had more in mind than buying party supplies. She clearly wanted to get Marco alone, and the way they looked at each other made Ana's heart swell.

"So we're all making tamales?" Chance interrupted, making Ana and Lucia laugh.

"Oh, Chance, you have no idea, but you will," Lucia said as they left.

"Wow, that was an unexpected twist, those two getting together. Hard to imagine that they waited all of those years."

"Well, things happen when they are supposed to sometimes, I guess," Ana said with a sigh.

Chance was watching her closely. Very closely. A tiny shiver worked over her spine. She couldn't help but focus on him with a sense of anticipation.

It was the New Year, and she would be spending it here, at home, with her family—and Chance. Sometimes, Ana thought, things worked out exactly as they were supposed to.

LUCIA SMILED, FEELING PURE happiness for the first time in her life. She ran her hands over Marco's broad chest, burying her face in his neck as she pinned him to the truck seat. He was hard and thick inside of her, filling her, and she moved, making him groan. His hands slipped through her hair to bring her mouth back for a kiss.

"The store will be closed by the time we get there, *querida,*" he said lightly, laughing and then catching his breath as she rotated her hips in a way that she had quickly learned made him crazy.

"I know the owner, and if I promise to have sex with him, he'll let me in after hours," she said, nipping at Marco's ear and dragging his hands to her breasts.

They'd pulled off the road to a quiet spot where no one would see them. Lucia had given Marco little choice in the matter, going down on him as he drove. She'd always fantasized about doing that.

Her muscles clenched around him as he took a hard nipple into his mouth and she watched, her shirt pushed up, her skirt up around her thighs. She moved over him. So wanton, so incredibly hot, she thought, a rolling climax thrumming through her, making her clench him tightly inside as she held his mouth to her breast.

"Oh, Marco, so good," she breathed, knowing he was close as he broke away, his head falling back. His eyes veiled as he watched her cover herself with her own hands and increased their tempo.

"So big, so hard inside me. I want you to come, *mio,*" she said, her voice shaking as she started to crest again, as well.

They'd made love on the beach that morning, when he'd told her everything, and stayed there, having each other over and over again until they'd had to leave.

Lucia wanted everything with this man. She would take every drop of pleasure she could from him, every second they could steal before this was over.

But maybe…it would not be over. Not forever.

She watched his face contort in pleasure as he lifted off the seat, pressing up into her as he chanted her name through his release. He filled her, and she rode out one more climax, falling against him, panting, spent.

For the moment. There would be more. As much more as she could have. She was unapologetically greedy. He had to leave her when this was done, when Ana was gone. She accepted that. They would be back together again someday—of that she was sure.

He kissed her deeply, lovingly, his lips firm and soft, his tongue rubbing lazily over hers. He pulled back and looked up into her face.

He was so handsome. So brave.

"I love you, Lucia. You should never doubt," he said. "I've always loved you."

"I've always loved you, too, Marco. I wondered if Ana was right, if we shouldn't have just come together sooner, but it seemed so impossible."

His eyes became more shuttered, and she felt him pull away from her, physically and emotionally.

"I wish I could offer you more, *cara*. But I cannot. Not now. And I don't expect you to wait again."

Lucia lifted from him, missing the heat and the fullness of him in an almost painful way. Straightening her clothes, she stared at him from the other side of the cab.

"I will wait. When you can come to me, I will be there. I don't want anyone else, Marco."

"You are too beautiful, Lucia. Too vibrant, too perfect to waste away alone, waiting for me."

A small smile played on her lips. "I may not be alone."

He frowned. "Well, yes, you will have your family, I know, and your work, but I meant that you deserve your own family. A husband. Children," he said, and she didn't miss the pain in his eyes as he said the words.

"I know what you meant, Marco. We are on the same page, as they say," she said somewhat vaguely but felt an excited stirring inside her. It could already have happened.

"Lucia, what are you—" He stopped, seeming confused, and then his face went blank. "We... I assumed you had, since you told me not to use anything last night..."

Lucia knew she should have told him she wasn't on any birth control. Why should she be? Her few lovers over the years had taken care of that, and keeping up a prescription wasn't exactly easy when she was traveling all over Central America. Besides, she knew, the minute he had come to her the night before, what she wanted. It was all she'd ever wanted.

"I love you, Marco. I know you have to leave, but I want this. I want this so much I can't even tell you," she whispered, shifting in her seat to appeal to him.

Shock was evident on his face, and he stared out the window for long moments, then faced her.

"You knew you could get pregnant?"

"I hope I already am. And if not, I hope we'll keep trying, for at least as long as you're here," she said, smiling.

His chest seemed to broaden even more with deep breaths, and his eyes were dark.

"How could you do this, Lucia? To conceive a child when the father cannot be here to raise it? How will this look to our families and our friends? I cannot quit the work I'm doing now, but I cannot leave you here if you are carrying my child. Was this the plan? A trap? A way to keep me here, even though I told you I must go?"

She drew back, hurt as if he had slapped her. "No! Marco, no. I have actually been thinking about this for some time, that I would adopt or find a way to have children on my own. I didn't want any other man, and then, there you were, in my room last night. And it was everything I wanted—almost. I know you can't stay, but I can wear your ring, and we can let our engagement stand, and even if there is a child, we'll wait for you, for when you can come back and be with us."

He shook his head. "And I will miss it all? Miss raising my own son or daughter? Have them know, so young, that I wasn't there? That is the kind of father you would make of me? Unnecessary? You should have found some sperm in a catalog and have done with it, Lucia," he said unkindly and started the truck, backing out of the spot too fast, hitting a bump that jostled them both hard.

"I—I'm sorry. I will take you to the store and then home. Make what excuses you must, but I will not be able to be with you again. I will leave tomorrow."

"Marco, no," she pleaded, her heart breaking, her eyes dumping heavy, hot tears. "Please, can't you see how good this is? How right?"

He looked at her, and pain and derision were scrawled all over his face.

"No, I'm sorry, Lucia. I cannot. All I can see is how the woman I thought I loved is more selfish than I ever would have believed."

Lucia felt her world implode, and curled up, trying to hold it together.

Perhaps this was how it was supposed to be. Maybe she was carrying Marco's baby already, and if so, she would have it and love it as she had always imagined. She would stay with her mother for a while and raise the baby in her family, and hope that someday, maybe, Marco would come back to her, because that hope was all she had.

# 11

CHANCE KNOCKED GENTLY on Ana's door and, when there was no answer, turned the knob and let himself in. She'd said she was okay to clean up on her own, but he'd noted the shadows under her beautiful eyes and the tension pinching near her mouth. She was tired and upset. And rightfully so.

He felt marginally better that she'd agreed to stay at the house for the remainder of her stay, but he couldn't shake the feeling that they were up against something far larger than he'd originally thought. And that Marco was somehow involved. It was a gut instinct, but there was just something about the guy. Chance was waiting on a call from Garrett or Jonas, the two digging to see what they could turn up.

It was all he could do for the moment.

"Ana, are you here?" he called and then saw that she was curled up on the lounge on her veranda, sleeping.

Chance crossed the room, squatting down by the side of the lounge, utter tenderness overwhelming him as he took in her face as she slept. She looked peaceful, her cheek snuggled down into her palm, long lashes brushing her skin as she breathed softly.

He didn't say another word, didn't touch her, though he wanted nothing more than to pull her in close to him, cover her and protect her from everything that could hurt her. If anything had happened to her—more than what did—he wasn't sure he could have treated it like a professional loss.

His feelings for Ana were ranging deep into the personal, stirring up things he'd never felt for any woman before. The thought of losing her was… Well, he didn't intend to let that happen.

Nodding to himself, as if reinforcing his own promise, he stood and started to walk away, letting her sleep.

"Chance?"

Her sleepy voice caught him like a net and drew him back.

God, she was so beautiful, it socked him in the gut just to look at her.

"Hey. I didn't want to wake you," he said, returning to her side. "I just came in to make sure you were okay."

"I was going to shower and change, but then I thought I would lay down, just for a few minutes. What time is it?"

"Not late. Only about an hour since we parted ways downstairs. Your mother must be taking out her anxiety in the kitchen—something is smelling really good down there."

Ana smiled and pushed up to sitting, looking much better than she had earlier.

"That is a well-known tradition in our house, to cook through just about anything, happy or sad," she said with a smile. There was more color in her face, more energy in her eyes, Chance noted with relief.

"How's the arm?"

She moved her shoulder, wincing a bit. "Better than earlier. Still very sore, but the throbbing has passed, thank goodness."

"It will heal quickly. Don't worry. Luckily, it really was just a scrape, though I know it feels worse than that."

Ana shuddered. "It does, but it's also the idea that a bullet did this—and what it could have done. If this little scrape feels like this, I can only imagine what it's like to actually get shot," she said, shaking her head.

Chance grimaced. "I don't intend for you to ever have to find out."

Ana's eyes widened. "You've been shot?"

"Once. Something I would rather not repeat."

"Where?"

Chance paused and then stood, unbuckling his belt and drawing down his khakis to show her where he'd once caught a twenty-two slug just below his hip.

She focused on the small scar and reached out to touch it, her fingers sparking lust as they ran lightly over the puckered spot.

"Someone shot you," she said, repeating it to herself, as if needing to convince herself it was true. Raising her eyes to his, she asked, "Why?"

He smirked. "Boiled-rabbit case," he said, and she frowned, shaking her head.

"Ever see *Fatal Attraction,* the movie?" he asked, and she nodded in immediate understanding.

"It's how the guys and I refer to it, jokingly, that case. A very wealthy trust-fund guy had one wife and too many girlfriends, and he'd broken it off with one of the lovers who didn't want to let go. So the wife hired us to protect him," Chance explained.

"Magnanimous of her, considering," Ana said.

"Yeah, well, as it turns out, it was just a cover story. She was the one who tried to shoot him, figuring one of the girlfriends would take the blame and she'd get all the insurance," Chance said. "But this was the only time I was shot, and it did hurt like a bitch," he said, shaking his head. "I couldn't ski or climb for almost a year."

She smiled. "So what did you do instead, to settle your adventurous spirit?"

He wasn't going to tell her that he'd gotten particularly close with his physical therapist, but opted for a partial truth.

"I worked on the plane, mostly, and did some other light activity. It was one long year," he said with a shake of his head.

"I can imagine. You like to take risks, to push yourself," she observed, running her fingers up and down the length of his hip now and sending sparks along his skin that made it hard to focus.

"Ana, I can't think straight when you touch me," he admitted, but didn't want her to stop.

"Good. I like that," she said, curving her hand around his backside and squeezing.

Chance was hard in three seconds flat, but backed away from her exploring hands. It wasn't easy, as he would have rather gotten closer.

"We shouldn't. Your arm," he said, taking a deep breath and pulling his shorts back on.

"My arm is fine. Just a little sore. I feel better now that the meds have worn off and I had some sleep. I could use some help cleaning up, though," she said coyly, looking up at him with those eyes. Chance couldn't look away, and he certainly couldn't say no.

He slid an arm around her, easing her up gently, careful not to touch her sore shoulder. When she stood next to him, he pushed the hair back from her face, kissed her forehead, her cheek, her jaw, before teasing her soft, soft mouth with his own.

This was different, he knew. Something was different.

"Your mother, she made that comment about her daughters finding good men," he said, nuzzling her.

"Oh, I'm sorry, yes... I mean, not that you are not a good man, but Mama, she sees wedding bells everywhere. I don't know how to tell her that we are, well, nothing serious," Ana said, sighing as she kissed the column of his throat.

Chance backed away slightly.

"So what are we, then?" he asked, shocked to hear himself ask the question that women had asked him over the years. His response was always to break it off and go in another direction as quickly as possible.

But he had no inclination to get away from Ana. Quite the opposite.

"What are you saying?" she countered, looking circumspect and...hopeful?

"Just that... I don't know. What I do know is that this isn't a job anymore for me."

She smiled. "Hmm, I'm glad to hear that. I'd hate to think you are this way with all of your clients."

He smiled, too. "I didn't mean it that way. Just that, yeah, this started as...fun. Attraction. A distraction, even. But it's more now. I'm not sure what, exactly, but I know I'd like to keep seeing you, even after this is over. If you'd like that," he said and realized he was actually holding his breath.

Chance had never once been nervous with a woman since sixth grade, when he'd asked Marlee Cooper out on his first date. She'd said no, and he'd quickly learned there were a lot more fish in the sea. Many, many pretty fish.

"I wondered if you felt it, too," she said, and he breathed again. "I'd like to keep seeing you, too. To see if we have…something," she said.

"Oh, honey, we definitely have something," he said with a smile, tipping her face up so he could let her know exactly how much something they had.

She parted her lips, meeting him kiss for kiss, the heat building rapidly between them. But when he inadvertently nudged her shoulder and she bit back a gasp, he sucked in a breath and stood still.

"I'm sorry, sweetheart. You make it hard to say no, but why don't we just focus on getting you cleaned up, change that bandage and we'll head downstairs to help your mom?"

He could see that she wanted to argue, but then she nodded. "Thank you, yes. That's probably best."

They made their way to her bath, where Chance helped her undress, and as it turned out, concern for her comfort far outweighed his need to make love to her…though his body was making its needs clear. He ignored it.

Her needs came first, and he helped her wash up in the shower, enjoying gliding the soft sponge over her skin, washing every curve and hidden space. He found the task to be oddly satisfying, still aroused—how could he not be? But just caring for her in this way satisfied something deep inside of him.

She grabbed his shoulder with her good hand as she balanced and he washed behind her knees, planting a kiss on her thigh.

"Chance, I don't think I can take this much longer," she said, her voice tight.

"Do you hurt? Do you feel sick?" he asked, cursing himself for getting too caught up in touching her.

She looked down, her cheeks flushed, her eyes glittering with heat.

"No, silly man. Your washing has put me at the edge. I need you to make me come, or I think my knees might give out if you keep this up," she said.

Her directness shot straight through him, challenging every ounce of control he had.

"I can do that. Can't have you falling, can we?" he said, looking up. She shook her head.

"That wouldn't be good, no," she agreed.

"Maybe this will be," he said, easing the sponge between her legs as he washed gently there, kissing the inside of her thigh.

Ana gasped, her fingers digging into his shoulder.

"Oh, yes, that is good," she said, panting as he continued to rub the sponge rhythmically along her sex.

"Maybe this will be even better," he said, dropping the sponge and parting her gently, replacing it with his lips, his tongue.

She was hot, slick. Even as the water ran down her body, Chance lapped at her clit until she cried out, and he didn't stop until she was sighing his name again. Her knees trembled, and he stood, pulling her into his arms to support her. He was as hard as steel, but he didn't care, rocking her back and forth as she relaxed against him.

They definitely had *something*.

"C'mon. Let's get that bandage on, and some clothes, and go make some tamales," he said, kissing her once and then stepping out of the shower, assisting her out, as well.

She laughed. "Have you ever made tamales?"

"Nope. Is it hard?"

"It's fun. Everyone pitches in. Like a factory. You're in for a treat," she said as they dried off and focused on her bandage.

Chance smiled as he affixed the bandage and helped her with her dress. He was pretty sure that as treats went, tamales were going to pull an easy second place.

ANA WAS HAPPIER THAN SHE could remember being in a very long time. The food was prepared, and she, Chance and her cousins were decorating the courtyard and the house. Tomorrow night, everyone would gather in the center of the village to watch fireworks set off over the water, exploding over the tree tops of the jungle, and then they would all travel from house to house for food and dancing, games and conversation.

But at midnight, she planned to sneak away and have a very private celebration with Chance, to bring in the New Year with him alone.

He wanted more. He said they had something. Ana had been thrilled to her bones when he had asked to see her after he was no longer her bodyguard. Then, he would just be…hers.

He'd cared for her so sweetly, so tenderly, her heart had just about burst earlier when he'd come to her room to help her. There had never been anyone like him, and Ana was romantic enough to admit there might never be anyone else who could make her feel this way.

It was too early, too brief, to tell him that she loved him—or that she could, so easily—but her heart insisted, every time she looked at him.

As if she had finally found something that she'd been missing all along, and she hadn't even realized it.

"What are you thinking about?" Chance asked her as he stood poised on a short ladder, holding up one end of some colorful garland that Juan was tacking into place from the other side of the entryway. Because of her arm, Ana couldn't help, except to direct their efforts, but she was having fun with that, too.

"Just that you need to move that a little farther to the middle," she said.

Her tone was innocent enough, but he got the message. She had asked him to move exactly that way, earlier, when his mouth had been on her in the shower.

His blue eyes darkened in response, letting her know he knew exactly what she was thinking about.

Ana smiled, looking away, enjoying the game. It had been so long since she'd played this way or had even flirted.

"I guess Lucia decided to stay at Marco's tonight," she said, checking the clock. It was unlike her sister not to call, but then again, it was clear that Lucia's focus was not on much other than Marco. Ana couldn't blame her, feeling much the same way about Chance.

"I guess so," Chance said noncommittally. Not that he would have much concern about her sister's love life, but Ana couldn't help but detect that Chance changed when the subject of Marco came up. His face would shift to a more serious and more neutral look, a mask—as if he didn't want to give anything away.

He couldn't possibly still be jealous of Marco having proposed to her—clearly, that was not even an issue. Marco and Lucia were a surprise, but clearly they were deeply in love. And Ana had eyes for no one but her bodyguard.

She smiled to herself; funny how only a few days ago she was doing anything she could to evade Chance, dead set against having a watchdog.

Now she was very, very glad he was so good at his job.

A cell tone sounded in the room, and she realized it was Chance's phone. He handed off the garland to another one of her cousins and excused himself to another room.

Ana couldn't help but wonder who it was. It had to be very late back in the States, and nighttime phone calls were usually important. Or perhaps a woman, a lover, making contact during his absence?

A jolt of jealousy was replaced with common sense; Chance was not that kind of man. But as he returned to the room, she could tell from his expression that something had happened on that phone call.

He walked directly to her, looking around the room, as if to make sure no one was listening.

"Can we talk in private for a moment?"

Ana frowned, wondering what was going on, and nodded. "Of course."

They went to the far side of the courtyard to a more private spot, yet she knew his request was not a personal one.

"What do you know about Marco? His past, what he's into?"

Ana was surprised by the question and took a second to process it.

"I don't understand—what do you mean?"

"I've just had a feeling about the guy. Something isn't right. He fights like he was trained to do it, and my gut tells me there's more there than meets the eye, so I had my brothers do some investigating," he told her.

"You had them look into Marco's background? But why? He works for his family business, in agriculture— that's all. What could he possibly be hiding? A lot of men know how to fight," she said, feeling as if Chance had perhaps become too paranoid.

"I think he probably does work for his family business, but I also think it's a cover."

Ana shook her head, waving off Chance's concerns. "A cover? A cover for what?"

"Possible illegal activity. Who knows? Maybe something else. All I know is that when Jonas and Garrett tried to dig up information on him, there was almost nothing to be found."

Ana stared at Chance, hands on her hips. "Maybe that is because there is nothing to be found—you are wasting your time on this, Chance. Marco is just… Marco. We've known him since we were children."

Chance didn't look as if he was buying it. "It's more than that. It's hard to explain, but when people are involved in things like illegal activity, or when they are working undercover, or in black ops—"

"Black ops?" Ana interjected incredulously.

"Or things like that. My brother Ely would know. He was one of them. Their records are often scant and clearly constructed—they have enough of a background to put them on the map, but sometimes, there's not much else. None of the things you find with normal, everyday life. Like travel records. Marco travels a lot, but there's very little record of where and for how long, where he stayed, that kind of thing."

Ana was completely confused, and she was, to be honest, a bit scared. Her sister was with Marco, and if Chance was right, what did that mean for Lucia?

"I don't know what to say. I've been away so long,

I don't know what's going on, but if you're right, is Lucia safe?"

"You should call her. Tell her your mother needs her home and wants Marco to come here, too. Make something up, but get them here. I'll feel better with her here and I'm going to talk to him myself," Chance said.

Ana could tell by his tone that he was dead serious, and while her mind told her that there was no way this could be true, concern for her sister and a willingness to trust Chance had her reaching for her phone.

"She isn't picking up," Ana said, and her hands trembled slightly as she dialed Marco's number.

Gratefully, he answered. Though he sounded odd— as if he had been drinking.

"Marco, thank goodness. This is Ana. May I talk to Lucia? Mama needs to check on something," Ana said, surprised at how normal her voice sounded.

No response.

"Marco? Are you all right?"

"I'm sorry, Ana, I was sleeping, and just getting my bearings. Are you saying Lucia is not there with you?"

Ana's hands turned cold.

"No. I thought she was with you," Ana said and gripped the phone more tightly. "Marco, what happened? Where is Lucia?"

"We had a fight. She took my truck home, but that was hours ago. Perhaps she stopped to walk along the shore, to think."

"No, she's not answering her phone. She wouldn't not pick up for me. Marco, what happened? What did you do? What did you fight about?" Ana asked, her voice increasingly louder and panicked in fear for Lucia.

Chance took the phone from her hands.

"Marco, what's going on?"

The men talked for a few minutes more, and Chance hung up.

"What did he say?"

"He's leaving now, going out to look for her. He said she was upset and didn't want to stay with him, didn't want him to take her home, so he lent her his truck. He hasn't heard from her since, but he's going to search for her and will call us back shortly."

Ana grabbed Chance's arm. "We need to go, too. She could have had an accident, if she was upset, or she could be hurt," she said, her throat constricting. She wasn't sure she could breathe, thinking about her sister hurt, or worse, while they had been here having such fun.

Chance took her face in his hands. "Ana, you need to stay calm. It could be okay, and we're going to find out. We have to stay put—this could be a trap to lure you out."

"I don't care! This is my sister!"

"I care, and you have to trust me, okay? We'll find her, and we'll settle this."

Ana wanted to fight, to run to her car and leave, but she also knew he was right.

"I will call the hospital, the police, to see if there were any accidents," she said, feeling sick at the thought.

"That's a good idea. Go. I'll let you know as soon as Marco calls," he said and pulled her in close first for a hug. "It will be okay. I'll make sure of it," he told her. Ana held on, pressing her face into his chest, wanting to believe him.

She did what she said she would, avoiding her cousins and not wanting to worry her mother. She went back to her room to call. A short while later, she didn't know if she was relieved or not that no one had been reported hurt in any car accidents, at least, no one matching Lucia's ID or description.

As she was going downstairs to tell Chance, he opened the door and walked through, and to her surprise, Marco was right behind him.

"Did you find her? What happened?" Ana asked, rushing across the room to meet them both.

Chance curled his arm around her and pulled her into his side, supporting her. He glanced down at her, his expression fierce.

"We will, Ana. You have to be sure of that."

She focused on Marco, her heart sinking. "What do you mean, we *will?* Where is she?"

Marco nodded, looking bleak but also angrier than she had ever seen him.

"I found the truck. With a note. They took her," he said, his jaw tightening. "And I will do whatever it takes to get her back. This is my fault, Ana, and I'll fix it. No matter what."

# 12

"LUCIA IS *PREGNANT?*" Ana hissed as she stood up from her seat in the courtyard, poised as if she were about to launch herself at Marco. Chance had no doubt from the look on her face that she wanted to hurt the man.

"No, maybe. I mean, she said she was hoping to be. We'd only been together for the last two days, but she wasn't... We didn't use..." He faltered, and Chance had to fight off a wince, embarrassed for the guy even if he had screwed up royally. "When she told me that, I didn't handle it well. I'm in the middle of this case, and I'm around some very dangerous people, and up to this point, it was possible to keep my lives separate. I told Lucia that I had to go back to my case, that I couldn't stay. Our engagement was..."

He paled, shaking his head as he met Ana's eyes.

"I love your sister. More than my own life. But our engagement was a sham. It was only an excuse for me to get closer to you, to have a reason to stay close while you were here."

Ana frowned. "Why?"

"The threat against you is coming from somewhere

within the group we've been infiltrating. I've done business with some of the fringe players, but we've been trying to get deeper, into the central management. None of the major players know me, and I thought it was best if I protected you myself—but it's hard to know whom to trust, and I think someone must have told them I was here."

"Wait, I don't understand," Chance interjected. "Are you saying you think someone from within the *federales* ratted you out to the criminals you were following?"

"It's the only thing that makes sense. The cartel itself would have no reason to follow me back here. But there is a price on Ana's head, and the police knew I was becoming engaged to her. It's possible that they mistakenly took Lucia, thinking that she was Ana."

Ana did step forward then and raised her hand to strike Marco's face. But she stopped, her hand dropping to her side. He never flinched.

"How could you? How could you do this to our family, to me, lying to us all? And sending Lucia away in the night, when you thought she could be pregnant? Because you had to return to your *job,* and you couldn't *deal* with it?"

Chance had seen Ana's passionate personality in many guises, but he had never seen her so purely angry. Electricity nearly crackled around her, and he set his hands on her shoulders before she forgot and hurt herself, her own wound still fresh.

Tears rolled unrestrained down her cheeks as she glared at Marco.

"If she dies, it will be because of you," she spat. "And because of me. If I had not come back, if I hadn't ignored the threats…" she said, her anger turning to guilt and defeat all at the same time.

Chance drew her in close. "No. This is no one's fault but the men who took her, and we'll find them. And we'll find her. I have my brothers working on tracing her cell. Marco, what do your people say? The ones you can trust, anyway? What do these guys want? What will happen when they find out that they don't have Ana, but Lucia?"

Marco seemed to wake up, responding to Chance's no-nonsense tone. They couldn't just stand around here arguing and crying, or Lucia would die.

"Two things. They will try to trade her, or…they will decide they don't need her around."

A strangled cry escaped Ana's lips, and Chance's heart squeezed painfully. He hated seeing her suffer like this, and he was hell bent on doing whatever he needed to in order to make her happy, as well as safe.

"Do you have any idea where they could be holding her?"

Marco was also clearly flat-out in love with Lucia and ready to hurt someone himself. Chance would be happy to help him, but it appeared he was going to be the coolheaded one around here.

"Listen, all that matters is finding Lucia. Do you have any idea where she could be?" he repeated.

Marco was quiet for a few beats, then looked up, shaking his head. "They could be anywhere."

Chance didn't like feeling helpless. It wasn't in his repertoire.

At that same moment, both his and Marco's phones rang, and they answered.

"Chance?"

"Jonas, do you guys have anything?"

"It's sketchy, but we may have a lock on Lucia's cell phone. I'm texting you the coordinates. It looks like it's in the middle of who knows where. Do you have anything from the police?"

"I'm standing here with one of their federal officers, and he's talking to his people now, I think."

"Good. Coordinate with them, and don't handle this yourself. These guys usually come in groups and they come heavily armed."

Chance nodded. "Copy that."

"How's Ana?"

"Upset, of course. Angry as hell," he said, watching her pace the courtyard a few yards away.

"Can't blame her, but it's even more important that you stick to her like glue, Chance. This threat was directed at her, and this could be a decoy, or who knows— this Marco, anyone, could be involved. Even her sister."

"No, it's not like that."

"You don't know. Believe me, I've seen worse. Just... stick with her. Let the police go find the sister."

Chance felt his spine stiffen. Sometimes his brothers forgot that he was an adult, completely capable of doing his job.

"Chance, we just want you home in one piece. Her, too, but this is nasty. Stay in contact, okay?"

Chance's annoyance dissolved when he heard the strain in his oldest brother's voice—they were worried. He knew his brother would send in the troops if he could, but they weren't in the United States, and Lucia was a Mexican citizen, and so was Ana, for that matter. There was nothing Jonas and Garrett could do but watch and try to help from afar. Chance knew how frustrating that could be.

"Don't worry, Jon. I don't intend to let anyone lay a hand on her."

There was a pause before Jonas simply said, "I see."

"See what?"

"Nothing, Chance. It happens to the best of us," Jonas said, and Chance shook his head at the phone. Why did everyone keep saying that to him?

"Okay, I have the coordinates," he confirmed, looking down at the incoming message. "I'll let you know what's happening," he said, cutting off the call.

"What did they say?" Ana asked both men as they converged on her.

"We have the coordinates on Lucia's phone," Chance said. "They could have ditched it, so we don't know for sure, but it could at least give us some direction on where they took her."

Marco's expression was dark, his eyes dangerous.

"We won't need them. I know where she is."

Chance understood immediately. "That wasn't the *federales*. That was whoever took her," he stated.

Marco nodded.

"They know they have the wrong sister, and they want Ana. They also want me."

"They know who you are? That you've been working undercover?"

Marco nodded. "I spoke to Lucia," he whispered, his tone choking. "I know she is alive. For now, but they said I have to come with Ana right now, or she won't be."

Chance swore under his breath.

"Okay, well, if we know where they are, can't you send in a team to get her out and apprehend these guys?"

Marco shook his head. "If they have someone on the inside, they'll know we're coming, and they'll kill her without a second thought."

"I will go. There is no time to do anything else," Ana declared, and Chance turned to her in shock.

"You're not going anywhere," he said and winced as he saw her eyes blaze. "I didn't mean it to come out like that, Ana, but you can't possibly go. They'll just kill you, Marco and probably Lucia, too. There's no benefit in you going. You don't think these people will really honor their word and let Lucia go, just because they said so?"

"Well, we have to do something!" she said, keeping her voice down. They had been trying to not alert everyone else in the house, especially Doncia, about what was going on. "I cannot take this. How will we save her?" Ana said, suddenly pale and lifting a hand to her shoulder.

"You're hurting, Ana. Have you taken any medicine?"

"No. I need to have a clear head."

"A couple aspirin, at least, won't muddy your thinking. I'll get you some," Chance said, turning to go inside.

"No, I'll get them. You two must find a way to work this out. There isn't any time," she said. She hugged Chance tightly and then headed toward the house.

Chance took a deep breath.

"They are independent women, Ana and Lucia," Marco commented. "Very passionate, very determined."

"You said it. So what next? I can't leave Ana here alone. This could be a trap. If we leave, she's here unguarded."

Marco pursed his lips. "I hadn't thought of that," he said. "You stay here, and let me see if I can pull something together."

"What are you thinking?"

"Ana and Lucia are very beautiful women, but we have some undercover officers who could look very similar to Ana, especially this time of night. If I can get one to go with me, with backup, we might pull it off."

"That's brilliant—but I thought you worried about whom you could trust?"

"It's getting too late for that now. We have to do something, so I'll just have to risk it," he said, pulling out his phone to make the calls.

It was Chance's turn to pace as he once again found himself feeling at loose ends, unable to help. But then Jonas's words came back to him; he had to focus. His job was the protect Ana—that was why he was here. As much as he wanted to help Lucia, he had to leave that up to Marco and the *federales,* and hope they could pull something out of their hats.

He supposed he should call Jonas back and let them know what was happening. Hed reached for his phone.

But it wasn't there.

Searching the ground around him, he couldn't find it, and panicked.

Ana.

When she'd hugged him, she must have lifted his phone. She had the coordinates for where Lucia might be, and she had the phone's GPS to use them. He heard the rumble of a car starting in the driveway, and cursed, running full speed to the driveway, only to see the brake lights disappearing down the dark road.

"Damn it," he yelled, Marco racing out to meet him.

"What happened?"

"Ana. She took my phone, and she took the car. She's going to try to go after Lucia herself."

Marco swore loudly. He'd driven his family's produce delivery truck to the house, his truck being stuck in the jungle where Lucia had been taken. The large, lumbering truck could never catch Ana in time.

"Doncia. She has a car out back. I can hot-wire it," Marco said, turning, only to find the woman he spoke of standing behind him, looking regal, as usual—and petrified.

"Or you can just ask me for the keys," she said. "You will find my girls?" she said, her eyes traveling from Chance to Marco and back.

"We will," Chance promised and hoped that he could keep it.

"Go, please. Please don't let them be hurt," she said, handing Marco the keys.

When he looked at her questioningly, she just said, "The courtyard is an odd place. Voices travel there. Even when you think you are not being heard, you are."

With that, she left them and walked back inside.

"Ready?" Marco asked Chance as they ran to the car. "I contacted my office, and they have someone meeting us there, though I don't know how Ana's going to affect the situation if we can't get to her in time."

"Then let's go," Chance confirmed as they sped out of the drive and down the dark road after Ana.

"You drive," Marco said, throwing him the keys. "I have to make a few more calls."

Chance hit the gas and pushed the cold fear in his heart back, knowing he couldn't even think about losing her. Losing Ana, and not having her in his life, wasn't an option. He'd do whatever was necessary to save her, even if he had to put his own life on the line to do it.

LUCIA SAT VERY QUIETLY ON the dirty floor in the corner of the dark barn, closing her eyes and trying not to think about it as she felt something run over her foot. Her hands were tied to post behind her, so tightly that they hurt, and her mouth was dry from the rag wrapped around her face.

Who were these men?

They had to be the group that Marco had infiltrated, that he was trying to take down. They might have seen her with him and thought this was a way to get leverage?

"Ha," she huffed through the gag, the effort making her choke. Her eyes burned with tears as she thought about him. He wouldn't even know she was missing, and if he did, he'd probably only be angry that she had messed up his undercover work.

She couldn't wipe the look on his face, or the words that he'd spoken, from her mind. The last moments she had with him—maybe her last moments forever—were angry ones. He didn't want to marry her—it was just a ruse for his job.

He certainly didn't want children or anything that would interfere with his work.

And now here she was because of his work.

How could she have been so stupid? She could be pregnant right now—so reckless, to have thought of bringing a life into the world and having it end like this.

Despair gripped her heart, and she tried to hold on, to *think*. The men had dumped her here and left her. She didn't know if there was anyone outside standing guard, but she didn't think so. She'd heard some cars come and go, and some voices, but that was all. Perhaps there was a house and she was just put here for safekeeping until they decided what to do with her.

They hadn't said a word, just laughed when she cried, asked who they were. They told her to shut up and hope that her boyfriend came through.

Came through with what?

Lucia had been trying to work the rope around her

wrists, but it was too strong. Her wrists were abraded from the rope.

What did it matter? What did anything matter?

Then she thought of the possibility of the baby—the baby that *she* wanted, even if Marco didn't—and started struggling again. Marco could go to hell. She was going to save herself, whether he came through or not.

Struggling more, she sobbed as she pulled at the rope, scoring her skin but not giving up. With one hard tug, she heard something rattle and then fall, making a crashing sound at the other side of the barn.

Lucia froze, scared to death of who might have heard the noise. Sure enough, the wide doors at the other side opened, and she saw the silhouette of one of her captors fill the doorway, an automatic weapon slung over his shoulder. He hit a light, making her blink at the sudden brightness.

"What the hell are you doing?" he asked in unaccented, perfect English. Not one of her people, not Mexican.

She didn't say anything, because she couldn't, but glared as best she could. Her struggles had knocked some copper buckets from a shelf. That was all.

The man was big—definitely white and mean-looking. He walked closer, squatting down by her and reaching out to touch her cheek.

"Were you lonely? You want some attention? I could help you with that," he said with a leer, smiling to reveal sharp, white teeth. He looked like a shark. A monster.

And she was helpless to defend herself.

A tear worked down her cheek as his hand drifted lower, and she closed her eyes, not wanting to think about where this was going.

"Such a waste. Might as well put you to some use

while we have you, right?" he said, taking his gun from his shoulder and laying it on the floor, reaching for his belt.

Lucia cried in earnest now, gagging on the cloth, wishing she hadn't knocked the buckets over. She didn't want to look, didn't want to see, and kept her eyes tightly shut, as if she could escape somehow through the dark she found there.

The next thing she knew, she heard a grunt, and the man's weight was on her, and she tried to scream, but realized something wasn't right—he wasn't touching her or molesting her; he was just lying there, and someone was saying her name.

"Lucia. Lucia, honey, it's me. Open your eyes," she heard a woman's voice whisper, and she did open her eyes to see Ana, the gun in her hands, the man at their feet, unconscious.

She had to be dreaming, and started to struggle, to fight, but Ana touched her face, calmed her down.

"Shh. You will make more of them come to check. Be quiet, and let me get you loose."

Lucia couldn't believe it; Ana was really here, really saving her.

It didn't seem real, but it was, as Ana released her hands and pulled the gag from her mouth.

Lucia coughed, moving her stiff, sore limbs as she stood.

"Ana, how…?"

"I had the coordinates for where they dumped your phone, not far from here. I followed tire tracks from there, all dirt roads, the idiots. I waited in the brush and heard the crash—I was coming in, but then saw the man come in first. I knew I had to move, knew he was going to hurt you," Ana said, taking the rope and tying it none to gently around the man's hands, and stuffing the gag into his mouth.

She grabbed the automatic weapon and handed Lucia the knife she had freed her with.

"Where did you get this?"

"I'm a cook," Ana said with a smile. "I knew I would need a weapon and took it from the kitchen before I left."

"But you are here alone?"

"I took matters into my own hands. You are here because you were mistaken for me. I wasn't going to wait around for everyone else to save you. But hurry. We need to go before someone comes to check."

Lucia nodded, gripping the knife in her hand, and then she grabbed Ana's hand, stopping.

"Ana, how did you know I was here?"

"Marco knew. I was calling to try to find you. Chance found out about Marco being undercover, or something like that. He told us you were on your way home, but we knew you hadn't made it. Things just... developed from there."

"So you are not alone? They are here?"

"No, I came alone."

"So...he would not come for me?" Lucia knew it was stupid, but her throat burned with the acknowledgment that Marco hadn't come to save her.

But Ana had.

"Lucia, we have to go. Marco was sick with worry for you, ready to kill them all, but I took it into my own hands and came myself."

"They don't know you are here?"

"They probably do by now," Ana said, grinning. Lucia, though she was crying, and so grateful, while still being scared out of her mind, also grinned.

"Okay, then, lead the way, my warrior sister."

The two women snuck out of the barn and along one side to the back, into the darkness of the jungle. Step by step, Lucia felt safer and calmer.

"Where is the truck?"

"Buried in foliage by the water. A few hundred feet that way." Ana pointed. The jungle was black and dangerous at night, but Lucia didn't care as long as she was out of that barn, away from the animal who was about to attack her. Better to be bitten by a snake or a panther than have suffered what he had planned.

As they got closer, Ana ducked down, pulling Lucia with her. Ana cursed under her breath.

"They found the truck. They are there by it. There's no way we can get close. We'll have to find a way to walk to the road, but they could have men in the area looking by now," Ana said worriedly. "Maybe it wasn't the smartest thing I did, taking off on my own," she added.

"Well, I'm just glad there are witnesses to that statement," Chance said from behind, startling her as she spun around, the gun pointed out.

"Whoa," he said, hands up, backing away. Marco did the same. "We're friendly."

Lucia's heart nearly burst seeing Marco, and she couldn't have been more shocked as he came toward her, wrapping her in his arms so tightly she couldn't breathe.

"Marco? What are you doing here?"

He finally let her go. "We found the truck abandoned and figured Ana had been taken, too. I guess we should have known better. We saw you come from the barn on the other side."

"Ana saved me. She was amazing," Lucia said, beaming at her sister.

"We're not out of here yet," Ana said grimly, her eyes meeting Chance's.

"Just stay low and wait. Help is on the way," he said. "And maybe give me or Marco that gun?"

Ana did and seemed happy to be rid of it. Lucia ducked down with them and was distracted by Marco's closeness; he touched her constantly, as if he couldn't believe she was right there.

Lucia looked over to her sister, who ducked down low with Chance, and saw their eyes meet, as well. Chance, however, held the gun, at full attention, his eyes on the surroundings.

Suddenly the sound of a helicopter overhead filled the night air, and voices and noises seemed to come from every direction. Lights glared, and Lucia and Ana watched as the Mexican police flooded the area, taking all of the men into custody, and she saw they had several men—including the one from the barn—held captive at gunpoint.

They were safe.

Marco led the way out of the jungle, and several police surrounded them, until they realized who they were, and then took Lucia to attend to her wounds. Ana shook off any help.

Lucia watched as the men were gathered up, and Marco helped his colleagues deal with them. Before long, he came over to where a medic had bandaged her up.

"You should get to the hospital," he said, checking her over closely.

"No, I am fine. Merely some scrapes and bruises."

Marco pulled her close. "I am so sorry. There are no

words for how sorry I am. When I found out you had been taken, I thought I would lose my mind," he said, his voice rough as he stroked her hair.

Lucia buried her face in his chest, inhaling his scent. "Why did they take me?"

"They thought you were Ana—they didn't know she had refused my engagement. When they saw you with me, they assumed you were her. I never imagined that could happen. I never would have put you in the line of danger, ever, but I almost ended up getting you, and perhaps our child, killed. I could never forgive myself," he said. "I love you, Lucia, and I was so wrong earlier. How could I even think of leaving, of going back to that, when now I have you?"

For the second time that evening, Lucia wasn't sure if she was dreaming. "I love you, too, Marco, and I was wrong. Wrong to do that, without your knowledge. I'm sorry, as well. I don't expect you to give up your work for me."

Marco nuzzled her cheek. "I'm giving it up for me, *cara.* All these years, you were all that I wanted, and then, when I had you, I pushed you away. What kind of fool was I? I won't make that mistake twice. Or ever again. You are mine now, if you'll still agree to spend your life with such a foolish, foolish man."

Lucia smiled as she cried and lifted her face for his kiss.

"I like that idea very, very much."

## 13

ANA FUSSED OVER THE DESSERTS as she helped her mother put out the food for New Year's Eve. It was hard to believe that just twenty-four hours before, she had been worried for her sister's life and crawling through the jungles to confront killers to free Lucia.

Now there was magic in the air as colorful lights twinkled everywhere, and all of her family and friends were dressed in their holiday best to celebrate. Ana had made her sister's favorite, the *caramel de leche,* and set it in the center of the table with a dozen other treats.

Later, they would walk down through the village and enjoy *ponche,* a hot drink made with *tejocote,* a fruit that tasted similar to apples. They'd watch fireworks and count down the seconds to welcome in the New Year.

A large, muscular arm slid around her shoulders and squeezed her close, being careful of her wounded arm. It had started bleeding again after her jaunt through the jungle, but it was a small price to pay.

"Marco," she said, smiling. "You startled me."

"These desserts look incredible, Ana. How could you do all of this in just a day?"

"I had plenty of workers, believe me. I can't take all of the credit, but quite a few of the recipes are from the new book and came out very nicely, I'll admit."

She stood back, pleased with her work, and took in her brother-in-law-to-be. He was every bit a classic, fantastically attractive Mexican man in his snug dark pants and cream shirt. Lucia was a lucky woman indeed, but Ana felt only sisterly affection for Marco, as always.

"You look so handsome, Marco. And happy."

"There are no words for it, Ana. To be here, to have Lucia... I feel like a new man. And to think how easily I almost turned my back on it all," he said, shaking his head. "If I had lost her—"

"Stop, Marco. She's fine, and the men who plotted all of this nastiness are behind bars. Hopefully forever."

Marco smiled. "Finding several kilos of cocaine in the back of that barn certainly helped boost the kidnapping charges. A lot of them were brought in, but the cartels are still operating, *cara*. You will have to be careful when you come here, unfortunately. Your celebrity status has made it dangerous for you."

Ana sighed, not wanting to think about any of that tonight. "Well, it's a good thing I will have a big, strong *federale* for a brother-in-law, then, isn't it?"

Marco arched an eyebrow. "And a trained bodyguard for a possible husband, perhaps?"

Ana choked on a chocolate she had popped into her mouth.

"Where did you get that idea?" she asked, catching her breath.

"Seriously, Ana?" Marco asked, his look telling her to drop the act.

"We're...attracted to each other. That's all. For now. Maybe we'll find more later, who knows, but neither one of us expected this or were looking for it, so it's day by day. I don't even really know him. Not really."

"I think you know what you need to know. He's a good man, willing to keep you safe, lay his life down for you if he needed to. And he's crazy about you. Take it from me."

Ana'a heart leaped with hope. She'd been keeping her expectations of anything with Chance in check, but seeing Lucia and Marco so in love and happy made it hard not to think of what if...

"We will see, I suppose," she said softly.

"As the man of the house now and as your new brother," Marco said sternly, jokingly, "it's my responsibility to make sure you find a good husband, if you haven't already."

Ana laughed. "I'll keep that in mind."

Lucia entered the room and joined them, looking striking in her red satin dress, accompanied by Chance.

When he walked in, he was all Ana could look at. He was dressed in a classic suit that took her breath away, and she smiled as she saw his tie—little chili peppers dotted the black background.

Lucia slid into Marco's arms, and Chance came to Ana, leaning down to kiss her cheek lightly.

"That dress is amazing," he said, taking her in. "I'll have to protect you from roving males for the rest of the night."

Ana felt her cheeks warm. "Thank you. I like your tie. And that's a beautiful suit," she said, returning the compliment.

Her thoughts before had been about the night's festivities, but all she could seem to think of now was taking that suit off of him and how she and Chance could make their own fireworks for the evening.

"Are you two announcing your engagement tonight?" Chance asked Marco and Lucia.

"We are, yes."

"When is the wedding?"

"We will go to a small church this week, with our families, and be married there. I don't want a big wedding, much to Mama's dismay," Lucia said, smiling. "That would take months, and I want to marry Marco as soon as I can."

"Mama will still want to throw a party, and you can't blame her. And I want to host a shower for you before I go back to the States."

"Oh, Ana, that is so sweet, but there is no need. There has been more than enough excitement."

"Perhaps a honeymoon in the states, then? There are such pretty places in the northeast. I think you would love Vermont in winter," Ana offered. "Please don't say no. My gift to you."

Lucia and Marco hugged her in thanks and then excused themselves to go mingle with guests and share their good news.

"How is your shoulder?"

"It's much better. A few glasses of wine have helped, and all of the good cheer," she said, feeling truly happy and relaxed for the first time in days.

"I have some good news," he said as he sipped a beer.

"Oh?"

"They caught your stalker. Turns out, we've killed two birds with one stone."

"Really? How so? Who was it?"

"Some sleazebag that Lionel hired to try to intimidate you and throw you off your game. So your instincts were good about him."

"How did they catch him?"

"Apparently the guy he hired was trying to shake him for more money, and Lionel refused to pay. So he went to the police and told them all about Lionel."

Ana's eyes went wide. "So the man who was stalking me, who was hired to do it, won't he go to jail?"

"He didn't actually walk into the police station and give himself up," Chance explained. "He tried to do it anonymously, but then the evidence added up, and Lionel ended up telling the police who he hired. No doubt Lionel's daddy will have expensive lawyers to fight his battles for him. I don't know that he'd see any time, but he will be off of your show, and you can get a restraining order. Or you can just call me if he bothers you again."

Ana felt a tiny thrill at the protective tone in his voice and the way his eyes darkened as he said it.

"That is good news. I guess we can just enjoy the night, then, yes?"

"That was my plan. But I guess you won't need me here now, after all of this."

Ana blinked. "What?"

"The immediate threat here is over, and so is the one back in the States. The production company has told me I'm off the job as of today, and I know you need to stay for the wedding and the rest of your vacation…but I should probably head back."

Some of the shine of the evening suddenly dimmed for Ana.

"You're going back? When?"

Chance shrugged. "Maybe tomorrow, if I can get the plane out. Or the next day."

"Oh…well," she said, lost for words and not wanting to show how disappointed she was by the news, since he seemed as happy as a clam.

Disappointed. No. Ana's heart hurt, to think that Chance was just going to leave. The job was over. That was that.

She knew she was being ridiculous. They'd only known each other a few days, and he'd said they would see each other back in the States, right? He had a family and job to return to, as well—he couldn't stay here babysitting her for no good reason.

Except that she thought the reason might be that he felt the same way about her that she felt about him. She didn't know what that was, exactly, but it was… deep. Different.

"Ana?" he asked, shaking her out of her thought.

"Oh, I'm sorry," she said with a light laugh. "I was just thinking about it all. I'm sorry you have to go. It would have been nice if you could be here for the wedding," she said, amazed at how her voice could be so steady when her heart was aching.

"Yeah, but it sounds like mostly a family affair," he said. "I've never been much for weddings, though my brothers seem to be having one after the other—two more this year, with Ely and Garrett. Dropping like flies," he joked, and Ana found it a little difficult to laugh along.

"Listen, I have to help Mama for a few minutes in the kitchen to make sure everything is done. Meet you back out here in a bit?"

Chance closed in, leaning down to whisper in her ear. "Absolutely. I really want to spend tonight with you, Ana, and as much time as I have here before I go," he said, his lips touching her skin.

A part of her was angry, confused by how he could make her feel this way and then just walk away. But she wanted him so much.

Ana knew that whether she'd see Chance back in the States or not, she was going to spend this last night with him, and let tomorrow take care of itself.

CHANCE WATCHED ANA walk away, unable to take his eyes off the way the silky silver dress showed off her amazing curves. But there was something in her stride, something halting and stiff that suggested she wasn't happy.

He'd seen the flicker of disappointment in her eyes when he told her he was leaving—or maybe he imagined it, because she seemed fine with it. Truth was, the production company hadn't completely released him from his duties, but he'd had to ask to be replaced. Apparently the executives were still worried about Lionel, since he would be free and a restraining order didn't do much these days. Also, there was always the potential for future threats. Chance knew that Garrett was hoping they would get this job for entry into more regular celebrity-protection details, but he couldn't do it. Not anymore.

Not after last night.

When Ana had gone missing, and he and Marco had found the abandoned car, Chance thought he would lose it. His mind raced back to the time when he was a kid, and his mother had had a car accident—as it turned out, a minor one—but his father had no idea until he and all four boys had gotten to the E.R. Their mother was fine, but Chance still remembered how panicked his father had been, how pale, how fearful.

And then there was Logan and Jill. Another reminder

of how terrifying it was to give yourself over to someone else so completely that if you lost them, you lost yourself, as well.

When you fell that hard for someone, everything changed. Life changed, and you changed.

And then risk took on a whole new meaning. It wasn't fun anymore.

Chance had felt that fear when he thought the cartel had taken Ana as well as Lucia. All he could imagine was finding them both dead, and the thought wiped his soul clean, leaving only loss and pain.

He couldn't do it. He just couldn't. He liked his life, and he liked how he lived, and love changed everything. It was time for him to leave, before he got in any deeper.

Ana didn't need a bodyguard here now, and when she got back to the States, she could argue with some new guy who would follow her around.

But he was still going to be with her tonight and every minute that he could until he went. He'd allow himself this much, and then he'd go. He'd said they would get together in the States, but maybe that wasn't wise. He saw how Ana looked at her sister and Marco, and had heard Marco's comment about Ana finding a husband.

Chance just wasn't husband material. No sense in leading her on about that.

That settled, he walked along the buffets, sure he had never seen so much food in his life, and everything looked amazing. He couldn't wait to try it. This had to be the most elaborate and colorful New Year's Eve party he'd ever been to. Grabbing a plate, he spooned out some of the tamales he had actually helped make and also tried many of the other delicious dishes on the table.

Plate loaded up, he joined a table of Ana's cousins, who welcomed him enthusiastically. He sat, ready to celebrate, but for some reason the joyous conversation around him and the delicious food on his plate weren't doing the trick.

Something was missing.

Chance pushed his plate back and looked around the festively decorated room as the conversation danced around him, but he didn't hear any of it.

Where was she?

Excusing himself with a halfhearted smile, he strolled outside into the warm New Year's Eve, looking for the glimmer of Ana's silver dress, but didn't see her in the crowd.

Going back inside, he went to the kitchen and upstairs, his pace quickening as his chest tightened. Where was she?

He pushed back the panic. The danger from the cartel had been eliminated—right? She was just here somewhere, visiting with guests. He spotted Doncia chatting with a group of older women. Ana said she had gone to help her mother in the kitchen, but Chance saw no evidence of that as he approached their table.

"Señora, have you seen Ana?" he asked politely, smiling and greeting the other women briefly but politely.

Doncia shook her head. "No, Chance. I have not seen her since before dinner, but perhaps she is off chatting with friends. I'm sure she's here somewhere."

Chance didn't want to worry her needlessly. She was probably right. Still, his gut twisted with worry that all was not okay.

"Of course, thank you. *Feliz año nuevo,*" he added and turned away, his eyes scanning the courtyard.

No Ana.

Something was wrong; he could feel it.

Searching the upstairs again, he found Marco in the front yard.

"We have a problem," he said under his breath.

Marco's celebratory mood snapped to serious in a second. "What's going on?"

"I can't find Ana. Is there any chance that they sent someone else? Someone who was in the crowd, who might have slipped our notice?"

"That would be bold. After last night's incident, they wouldn't be looking for more attention from the law, but I suppose it's not impossible," he said, rubbing an agitated hand over his face. "We may have relaxed our caution too soon."

Lucia joined them, clearly curious about what was going on.

"Ana is missing. It could be someone who is still here, or there might be others, so—"

Lucia looked at them as if they were crazy. "Ana is not missing. She's right there," she said, pointing.

Indeed, Chance and Marco both looked across the winding driveway in front of the house, and there was Ana, holding a drink with both hands, talking to someone Chance didn't know.

Relief made his knees weak, and his heart hit hard against the inside of his chest as he closed the space between them.

"Where were you?" he demanded roughly, his tone creating shocked expressions on Ana's face and that of her companion, who offered a quiet excuse and slipped away.

Hot color invaded Ana's cheeks as she looked at him.

"Chance, what's wrong with you? You're being rude. I was just talking with an old friend, if you must know."

"I wondered where you were, and I searched everywhere and couldn't find you," he explained, feeling more like an idiot by the minute, but he couldn't seem to temper his reaction. "I thought someone had come after you again."

Ana blinked, as if trying to process what he was saying. "I'm sorry you worried. I went for a walk. I needed to think," she said.

"A walk? By yourself? That isn't safe," he said, knowing that on some level he was being irrational.

"I was fine. But guess what, Chance? Not everything in life is safe. In fact, a lot of the best things aren't. You of all people should understand that. Or maybe you are only willing to risk when there really is no risk at all," she said, her voice loud now, too. She raised her chin, facing off with him.

"What's that supposed to mean?"

"You will take on criminals, jump from cliffs, throw yourself out of planes or all of these other things, but you never really risk *yourself,* do you?"

It was his turn to be confused.

"I have no idea what you're talking about, Ana. Listen, whatever. I'm glad you're safe. I guess I was wrong."

"I guess I was, too," he heard her say under her breath as he turned away. Pausing, he stopped, turned back.

"What does *that* mean?"

She looked at him with her heart in her eyes, tears shimmering. Chance told himself it was anger. She was just angry at him for calling her out.

"It means that you can share your body—risk your

body, your safety—but not your heart. That is locked up safe somewhere, where no one can really touch it. I thought—" She stopped, closed her eyes, shook her head as if shaking something free. "Never mind. It does not matter. Your job is done here, Chance. Go home."

With that, she stormed away, leaving him speechless.

"You said we were nothing serious. You said it was only a fling," he called after her, surprised to hear the words come from his own lips.

But watching her turn her back on him had ripped him open. He should leave. He should go home. As he intended to do; as she told him to do. But he couldn't seem to move from the spot.

All he could think of was Ana and the gut-wrenching fear he'd felt watching her held at gunpoint in the cave. How afraid he had been when she went to save her sister. And how his blood had switched to ice when he hadn't been able to find her tonight.

*Fear.* Chance didn't like being afraid of anything, and with Ana, he had experienced fear more deeply than he had ever known.

She must have heard him, but kept walking, disappearing into the house.

People around him milled in the opposite direction, seeming oblivious to the drama, on their way to the center of the village to watch fireworks and count down the New Year.

Chance went to join them. Not to celebrate, just to leave.

*She doesn't want me,* he thought, the image of her walking away carved in his mind.

He didn't need this. Something, the incident with Logan, all of his brothers finding their wives and the holiday, Ana…it had all skewed his thinking. Nothing felt the same.

Nothing felt right. He had to leave, to get his balance back.

Walking down through town, he headed to the lot where they had parked their cars to get them out of the driveway for the party, and felt for his keys.

Damn, he'd left them at the house.

He would wait a bit, and when Ana joined her friends and family, he could go back, get his stuff and get the hell out. He'd fly back, find some friends. Maybe spend a few weeks going sport fishing or scuba diving. Something.

"She's right, you know," someone said behind him. Marco.

Chance turned, just agitated enough to want to fight with someone, and snarled at the big man.

"Mind your own business, Marco. You have no idea what you're talking about."

"Oh, I think I know a little bit about it," he said with an easy laugh as he joined Chance walking, matching his pace easily. "I realized, after the fact, that I was scared to death when Lucia told me she could be pregnant. I don't know that I had ever been that frightened in my life, until she was kidnapped. Then…" He took a breath, shoving his hands into his pockets. "Then I knew real fear. It's not easy for men like us to take, the fear. But I think the love can outweigh it."

"I'm not afraid," Chance said between his teeth. "This just…ran its course. I should have known better, anyway. I was distracted, and maybe if I hadn't been, none of this would have happened. We wouldn't have gone to the cave, she wouldn't have been shot. And if I had been on my game, she never would have gotten out of my sight that night and gone after Lucia," he said, cursing under his breath. "I've botched this entire job."

"Falling in love will do that," Marco said easily, kindly. "But the truth is that you protected Ana fiercely, and like her sister, these women are not going to be held back. They make their own decisions, and you cannot protect them from that. Maybe that is what scares you most of all," he offered.

"I'm not in— That's not what—" Chance sputtered, losing track of his thoughts, everything jumbled.

Marco turned, standing in front of him, stopping his progress down the street.

"Really? Then why the hell are you running away if you are not afraid? Look at you, heading out of town like a scared dog with its tail down," he scoffed, challenging.

The change in tone shocked Chance and really pissed him off. If this guy was looking for a fight, he'd come to the right place. Except that…as much as Chance's body stiffened, his muscles tightening, readying for a fight, his mind, everything inside of him seemed to collapse inward.

He cursed on the expelled breath that seemed to flatten him as he realized Marco was 100 percent right.

Marco put a hand on his shoulder again, as if knowing he'd won the round without throwing a single swing.

"You only have to ask yourself, Chance, if the fear is worth it. And if you think leaving and never seeing her again will truly make you happy. If so, travel well, my friend," Marco said with a slap to his back. "I must go find Lucia. We are bringing in this New Year, and all of the ones ahead, together."

Chance stood, again rooted to the spot, hearing the

cheering of the crowd, the blasts of fireworks in the distance.

He imagined never seeing Ana again. Never touching her, never arguing with her. He was walking away from the biggest adventure, the biggest risk, he'd ever faced. His father had once told him that if there was nothing to fear, then there was no real gain, either.

Real risk meant you might lose.

But it also meant you could win, big-time.

Chance had been taking acceptable risks—easy, predictable leaps that he controlled, that he could live with.

Until now. Losing Ana…the thought sucker punched him in the gut. Like Jill had almost lost Logan; like Garrett had lost his first wife, Lainey.

In the larger sense, he couldn't control it. Life was dangerous. But he could control losing her now by not walking away.

Maybe it was too late. She didn't want him; and he didn't blame her.

Even so, he turned and started heading back to the house. Glancing at his watch, and seeing it was only minutes to midnight, he broke into a run.

# 14

ANA WATCHED THE FIREWORKS from her bedroom balcony, but she didn't really see them. All she kept seeing was Chance walking away, leaving.

He'd called out to her, and she had kept walking.

What had she been thinking? She'd told him to go. So he went.

Why was she surprised? Because somewhere in her heart, hope had blossomed. Hope for the more that they had mentioned that day at the baths.

Tears fell even though she tried to hold them back, her hands curling around the wrought-iron rail of the balcony until they hurt. How could she feel this strongly about a man she had met only days ago and whom she had not even wanted in her life?

*How* had very little to do with love, her mother used to say when she was a young woman, and she had asked all the usual questions. *How long will I wait? How will I know? How come he doesn't ask me out?*

*How come I had to fall in love with a man who walked away from me so easily?* Ana thought, finally letting the pain have its way.

She thought when she challenged him, if she called him out, he would fight. He would deny what she said. He would tell her she was wrong and that he did want to take a risk with her.

Oh, well.

Ana returned to her room, intent on crawling into her bed and not coming out until the New Year. And until she could face her family without feeling like such a fool. Maybe, though, she would go downstairs and get some wine first...while the house was empty.

As she reached for the door, there was a noise outside and a hard knock.

"Ana? Ana? Open the door," Chance said.

She paused, silent. Shocked. Unsure.

"Ana, please. I saw you on the balcony. Please. Let me in," Chance said, something in his voice that made her reach for the door, open it.

"Ana."

Her name came from him on a sigh of relief—had he been afraid she wouldn't open the door?

"Chance, what are you doing?" she asked, passing her hand under her eyes discreetly, hoping her tears didn't show, but then she remembered he'd said he'd seen her from the yard.

"I..." He stopped, looking as if he was searching for words. He had clearly seen her crying and was trying to...what? Assuage his guilt so that he could leave with a clear conscience?

"There's no need for apologies, Chance. Goodbye," she said wearily, deciding to make it easier on both of them. Then it hit her that he could only have seen her crying if he had *come back.*

"I love you," he said, so quickly, so nervously, that she wasn't sure she had heard it correctly. Then he repeated, "I love you. At least, if this isn't love, since it's only been a few days, I'm pretty sure I'm on my way there, and fast," he said with a lopsided grin. "Maybe we could find out, though?"

Ana wasn't sure she'd heard him right and stood there in silence, uncertain what to say. Her heart was telling her to throw herself at him, to tell him she loved him, too, but her head was too busy arguing.

Chance stepped forward.

"Can you forgive me for being a jerk? I was...afraid. I've seen people fall in love and lose and be wrecked by it. I guess I thought it was a risk I didn't want to take, but then I met you. Now I know it's worth it."

Ana heard an indistinguishable sound come from her lips, and too much emotion welled up, making words inadequate. Her heart, however, told her exactly what to do.

She nearly knocked Chance over as she threw herself into his arms and met his mouth for a desperate, hot, then consuming, completing kiss.

She held him so tightly, making sure he was actually there, saying the things that she couldn't even imagine. Suddenly, the sound of the fireworks outside filled the air, and she knew it was midnight.

The New Year, a new love.

"Ana?" Chance whispered against her lips. "I guess this means you forgive me?"

"Only if you forgive me back," she managed, reaching past his shoulder to close the door behind him.

Chance pulled back. "Forgive you for what?"

"For walking away first. You called out to me, and I didn't answer. I told you to go," she said, holding his face in her hands, wondering how she could have ever been so stupid.

"I'd told you I was leaving earlier. I knew it then, that it was wrong, but when you took off after Lucia and when I found the empty truck, I… It was the only time in my life that I had ever been that afraid. I thought it was a bad thing, something I needed to avoid, to get away from. But I don't want to get away from loving you, Ana. Though I do wish you'd take fewer risks," he said, and she laughed.

"This! Coming from you!" she exclaimed, sheer joy suffusing her as she teased him. "Maybe we should take our risks together, Chance. Keep each other as safe as we can. I'm willing to put my heart in your hands. I love you, too," she said, the words she hadn't said to any other man falling very easily, surely, from her lips.

He led her toward the bed, his mouth coming down on hers, exploring. She opened to him completely, not wanting to hold anything back, and hoping he wouldn't, either.

The way he touched her, hands everywhere, unzipping her dress, sliding over her skin, as she undressed him as well, told her that they were both finished with holding back. From now on, they would take every leap together.

"Hey, what do you know…it worked," he said, his eyes drifting down over her.

"What?" she asked breathlessly as his lips brushed her earlobe, nipping, then her throat, and lower.

He stopped, sliding a finger under the clasp of the lacy red bra she wore—matching panties, as well—and it hit her.

"The red… I guess we both got our New Year's wish," he said, letting the material slide from her body as he came up to kiss her fully. "Happy New Year, sweetheart," he said.

"Happy New Year, Chance. Something tells me it's going to be the best one ever," she whispered before he kissed her again and made the rest of her wishes come true.

# *Epilogue*

*Six months later...*

THE BERRINGER BROTHERS SAT around the conference room table, watching the latest episode of *Ana's Kitchen*. Chance had told them they all had to see the premiere, and no one was arguing.

"She looks happy," Jonas remarked, and Chance nodded.

"Getting out of the reality TV show was a good decision. This makes her happy, and the show has taken off. She has complete control, though, and does it her way."

"Knowing Ana, I can't imagine anything else," Garrett commented.

"You've got that right."

"I can't believe you got married in Mexico," Jonas said, shaking his head. "But it sure agrees with you. You look happy, bro."

Chance grinned. They'd seen no reason not to make it a double wedding with Lucia and Marco.

"You know me. I like to jump right in," Chance said, knowing that the leap he'd taken with Ana was one of the best risks he'd ever taken in his life. "Listen to this part," he said, making his brothers stop talking and pay attention.

"Today's show focuses on food for children," she said, "and how to include your children in your cooking. I became a cook because my mother and my aunt taught me how to work in the kitchen since I was very small. It's a good way to bond with your children and to teach them to cook for themselves, as well as a way for them to exercise their creativity. I look forward to cooking with my own children very soon," Ana said, making eye contact with the camera in a way that seemed to look right out at them.

All three of his brothers turned to Chance, who sat grinning, waiting to see how long it would take them to get it.

"Uh...does she mean what I thinks she means?" Jonas asked.

"Hell, Chance, I haven't even made it down the aisle yet, and you're going to be a dad?" Garrett said, his own wedding still a month away.

Chance shrugged, bringing out a nice bottle of tequila that he'd gotten south of the border specifically for this occasion.

"What can I say? Ana and I both like an adventure," he commented. "Lucia will be due around the same time, so it's nice the cousins will be close in age."

"That's just amazing, man," Ely said, wrapping his youngest brother in a bear hug.

"Thanks. I wouldn't have seen it coming, either, but Ana's the best thing that's ever happened to me. Too bad Luke couldn't be here. I'll have to call him to let him know," he said as his brothers congratulated him with a toast.

"Where is he, anyway?" Ely asked, having been

away in Montana for several months. "Everything going okay with him?"

"He's gotten up to speed quickly, and we're picking up more white-collar gigs," Garrett said. "He was acting strange the other day. Asked for some time off, said he needed to go help a friend. It was all he'd say. It seemed like something had shaken him, but he wouldn't say what. Didn't want to talk about it, I guess. I told him to go, take whatever time he needed."

"I wonder what's up," Jonas said and then shrugged. "Luke always was a little different. In a good way, but sometimes he's hard to figure. And he's been through a lot. Better now, but maybe you never get over that kind of thing."

Chance nodded. Luke had everything at one time—wealth, fame, his own investment firm—until one of his employees had lost their job and committed suicide. He'd sold it all then—his shares in his company, his houses, his cars, every last bit of it—and had disappeared for several years. But he'd gotten past that difficult phase. Healed, or seemed to, anyway.

"Well," Chance said, "as long as he knows he's one of us now, and we watch each other's back. Whatever he needs, we'll be there."

The brothers raised their glasses to that, to all of their futures and all of the adventures that were surely coming their way.

LUKE BERRINGER HAD BEEN sitting outside the school for hours. Days, actually. It didn't make sense, finding her here, but this was where the online trace had brought him. Only Nicky Brooks would run a scam from inside an elementary school. She'd probably hacked into their computer system. Brilliant, really—the FBI didn't tend to look for thieves who used fourth graders' computers.

She had to show up sooner or later. And when she did, he'd have her.

On a silver platter, ideally.

Nicole—Nicky—Brooks was back. He'd been waiting for years for her to pop up on the radar somewhere, and finally, there she was. A glimpse of her on the airport facial-recognition software that Luke's former company had created had pointed him in the right direction.

Luke wondered how long she'd been in Tampa. Had she been this close, practically right under his nose, all along?

Six years since she had slept with him, lied to him and stolen from him.

He'd known about the lying—he just hadn't cared, as she was fantastic in bed. So she hadn't used her real name? So what? A lot of people had secrets, and they had their reasons. He wasn't marrying her; it was just about the sex. Or so he'd thought. For Nicky, it was all about the access.

Oldest trick in the book, and he'd fallen, hook, line and sinker.

But the stealing, that was another thing altogether. She'd stolen information from the company he'd owned then—information that someone else had been blamed for stealing.

It had ruined a life. Taken a life.

Luke's fault, because he hadn't looked deeply enough until later. As he'd dug into the theft, he'd found who had really committed the crime.

And she was long gone.

So he'd waited. Set traps, gone about his life.

He knew he'd find her one day, and he'd make sure she paid.

"And there you are," he said to himself, watching as she finally walked out of the building, sexy and confident as ever. In black pants and a white blouse—not exactly high fashion for Nicky—yet she was still all long legs and sexy swagger.

He felt his body respond and harden—it was difficult not to react to the sight of her, though he told himself it was just the anticipation of bringing her down. Making her pay. He was going to send her to jail, and he had the proof to make it happen. Only then could he truly make peace with the past.

"What scheme are you running now, Nicky?" he said softly in the empty car as he eyed her approach a snow-white Mustang parked near the curb.

Nicky always had style. He'd give her that.

Though that style was sacrificed to whatever scam she was running, it appeared, as she headed instead across the small lot to her car, a Toyota that had seen better days. Nicky loved hot cars, and it must be killing her to drive that pile of scrap, he thought with a small smile. Whatever it was she was after, she must want it bad. A long con of some sort to put this much work into her cover.

Pulling out of the lot, she headed down the palm-tree-lined street, and Luke waited a few seconds, then pulled out behind, following.

They headed down busy streets, through several lights and turns over the causeway out of the city, until Luke thought perhaps she'd made him and was trying to lose the tail. Then she pulled into the short driveway of a small block home at the edge of the intercoastal and got out of her car. Sighing, she looked tired as she reached in the back and hauled out her large bags, tugging them over her shoulder and heading to the door.

The cottage was cute, probably a rental. Totally not her style. Whitewashed cinderblock encased big windows and a terra-cotta roof that had a lot of charm, especially with the two towering palm trees providing shade in the front yard, but not much luxury. Whatever Nicky was up to, she was lying low.

Well, the jig was up. Luke got out of his car. He wasn't going to risk having her slip from his grasp one more time.

As he crossed the street and approached the house, he noted the name Grant on the pelican-shaped mailbox and smirked. Was she stealing someone's real identity? Someone who actually lived here but was out of town?

But then a neighbor emerged from the yard next door, an older woman who smiled and called out to Vanessa, and Nicky turned, bestowing a smile on the woman. They started talking about something that Luke couldn't make out, and he walked down the side of the Toyota to wait behind the corner of the house until Nicky was alone again.

Just then, Luke noted the wire that ran across the inside of one of her windows…and the tool marks on the sill that showed someone had come in and out through that entry point.

The wire came from the top of the window down to the sill, and appeared to head toward the door. Luke had seen that type of wiring before, and his mind stilled as he looked through the window and noted what looked like two bricks taped to the walls inside the door, attached to the wire.

Luke cursed.

As he heard Nicky call out a goodbye and thanks to her neighbor, he turned the corner of the house.

"Nicky!"

She didn't seem to hear him, intent on opening the door as she picked up her bags and once again started to insert her key into the lock on the door.

He heard the click, heard the turn of the knob as she opened it and then the whoosh from inside as he ran up the steps and tackled her, pulling her over the railing with him. They both landed hard on the grass, but they were still too close.

"What—" she gasped, wincing as he pulled her roughly up. They only had seconds, literally, as the door swung open. Maybe less.

"Nicky! Nicole, *move,*" he ordered when she didn't move, pulling her from the grass and making her run with him down past a cement wall where they could take cover.

Damned if anyone was going to kill her before he got her to jail.

The blast was deafening and knocked them both flat, heat searing the air around them as the house went up in a mass of flames.

The heat receded, and Luke rose, taking a look, and heard the sirens just a second later.

Nicky lay on the cement, scraped, pale and staring in shock.

"What the hell is going on, Nicky?" he asked, sitting up. Sirens screamed in the background.

She looked at him, pale and confused. He would have thought she was faking if the physical evidence wasn't there—the trembling, the pallor, the way her pupils were too dilated. Her breath was coming too fast, and he shook his head. Nicole had never been easy to shake, but maybe nearly getting blown up did the trick.

"Take deep breaths, try to calm down," he instructed harshly. "I need you to stay conscious, Nic, so you can make it to jail today instead of the hospital."

"Mrs. Shaw!" she yelled, as if she hadn't even heard him. She stood, running back toward the house. "Mrs. Shaw!" she yelled, and it took Luke a second to realize she must be calling out to her neighbor.

Nicky ran hazardously close to the flames as she raced inside the porch of her neighbor's home, and Luke followed.

"Oh, no," Nicky cried, finding the older woman passed out on the front yard.

"Let me see," Luke said harshly, pushing Nicky aside to check the older woman's pulse. "Her pulse is good, but call an ambulance, Nic."

She blinked at him, those big blue eyes clouding over. "Who are you? Why did my house explode, and why were you there, and why do you keep calling me Nicky?"

Luke barked out a harsh laugh. "Give me a break. Don't you remember me? Way to hurt a guy's feelings after the things we did together," he said, sending her a humorless leer.

Her cheeks showed the first signs of color, her eyes snapping.

"I don't know who you are or what you're talking about, but I know for sure I've never done *anything* with you," she said, outraged.

Nice act. The lack of recognition on her face was downright artful. Honed by years of practicing her craft of deception. Apparently she was going to play this to the end.

He nodded to the house. "Looks like someone else found you, just like I did. And as usual, more innocents left in your path, hurt because of what you do, Nicky."

She stood up shakily, looking at him as if he must be mad, shaking her head. Luke grabbed for her, but she was too fast, moving quickly down the sidewalk as police cars pulled up to the curb. In the distance, more sirens wailed, probably the EMTs. Luke stayed with the older woman, who had started to come to again, and he murmured something comforting to her as he watched Nicky talk to the cops.

She was beautiful, even with her less-than-glamorous schoolteacher look, and the police were happy to help. Of course. Nicky knew her way around a man like Marco Polo knew the Silk Road.

They wouldn't listen to him now, but he had proof that would make sure they listened later. An officer approached him.

"We'll need you to come to the station, sir. As a witness, of course," he said, but Luke could tell by his look that Nicole had already worked her magic, casting an aura of suspicion over him.

"No problem, Officer. Here are my credentials, and I'll be happy to cooperate in any way I can," he said, handing the man his license and his Berringer Bodyguard ID. "I think this young woman should be brought in, too, for her own safety. You're going to find that this explosion was no accident. I saw the wiring in the window just before she opened the door."

The officer looked at him, his ID and then at Nicole, who frowned. Luke met her confused gaze; whatever game she thought she could play, he could play better. He'd been thinking about this for years. Savoring the idea of the moment he could take her down.

As the EMTs arrived and took over with Mrs. Shaw, he waved away their concern for him, keeping his eye on Nicky as they examined her by the roadside. Her face was streaked with tears as the initial shock wore off and emotional response set in. If he didn't know the truth, he'd truly feel sorry for her.

But he did know, and when it came to Nicole, he didn't feel anything but the need for justice.

The police talked to her for a second, clearly informing her that she, too, would have to report to the station and ushering her toward a cruiser near the curb. Luke smiled and happily joined them. He didn't miss the look of outrage on her face as he opened the door for her to get into the backseat.

As he joined her, stretching his arm out along the back of the seat and watching her scrunch away from him, he pinned her with a look. She could only keep this act up for so long. Soon, he'd make sure that Nicky Brooks was put away for good.

\* \* \* \* \*

COMING NEXT MONTH FROM
# HARLEQUIN® BLAZE™

Available January 22, 2012

## #735 THE ARRANGEMENT
### by Stephanie Bond

Ben Winter and Carrie Cassidy have known each other forever. And they like each other—a lot! But when those feelings start to run deeper, Ben thinks he's doing the right thing when he ends the "Friends with Benefits" arrangement he has with Carrie. After all, he wants more from her than just great sex. It seems like a good plan...until Carrie makes him agree to find his replacement!

## #736 YOU'RE STILL THE ONE • *Made in Montana*
### by Debbi Rawlins

Reluctant dude-ranch manager Rachel McAllister hasn't seen Matt Gunderson since he left town and broke her teenage heart ten years ago. Now the bull-riding rodeo star is back and she's ready to show him *everything* he missed. All she wants is his body, but if there's one thing Matt learned in the rodeo, it's how to hang on tight.

HB0113CNMENHA

## #737 NIGHT DRIVING • *Stop the Wedding!*
### by Lori Wilde
Former G.I. Boone Toliver has a new mission: prevent his kid sister's whirlwind wedding in Miami. The challenge: Boone can't fly, so he agrees to a road trip with his ditzy neighbor, Tara Duvall. She's shaking the Montana dust from her boots and leaving it all behind for a new start on Florida's sunny beaches. It's one speed bump after another as they deal with clashing personalities and frustrating obstacles, until romantic pit stops and minor mishaps suddenly start to look a whole lot like destiny.

## #738 A SEAL'S SEDUCTION • *Uniformly Hot!*
### by Tawny Weber
Admiral's daughter Alexia Pierce had no intention of ever letting another military man in her life, even if he was hot! But that was before she met Blake—and learned all the things a navy SEAL was good for....

---

HB0113CNMENHB

Navy SEAL Blake Landon joins this year's
parade of *Uniformly Hot!* military heroes in
Tawny Weber's

# *A SEAL's Seduction*

Blake's lips brushed over Alexia's and she forgot that they were
on a public beach. His breath was warm, his lips soft.

The fingertips he traced over her shoulder were like a gentle
whisper. It was sweetness personified. She felt like a fairy-tale
princess being kissed for the first time by her prince.

And he was delicious.

Mouthwatering, heart-stopping delicious. And clearly he
had no problem going after what he wanted, she realized as he
slid the tips of his fingers over the bare skin of her shoulder.
Alexia shivered at the contrast of his hard fingertips against
her skin. Her breath caught as his hand shifted, sliding lower,
hinting at but not actually caressing the upper swell of her
breast.

Her heart pounded so hard against her throat, she was surprised it didn't jump right out into his hand.

She wanted him. As she'd never wanted another man in
her life. For years, she'd behaved. She'd carefully considered
her actions, making sure she didn't hurt others. She'd poured
herself into her career, into making sure her life was one she
was proud of.

And she already had a man who wanted her in his life. A nice, sweet man she could talk through the night with and never run out of things to say.

But she wanted more.

She wanted a man who'd keep her up all night. Who'd drive her wild, sending her body to places she'd never even dreamed of.

Even if it was only for one night.

And that, she realized, was the key. One night of crazy. One night of delicious, empowered, indulge-her-every-desire sex, with a man who made her melt.

One night would be incredible.

One night would *have* to be enough.

**Pick up *A SEAL's Seduction* by Tawny Weber, on sale January 22.**

# REQUEST YOUR FREE BOOKS!
## 2 FREE NOVELS PLUS 2 FREE GIFTS!

## red-hot reads!

# Rediscover the Harlequin series section starting December 18!

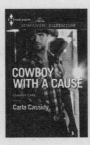